LETTERS BETWEEN GENTLEMEN

BY PROFESSOR ELEMENTAL
AND NIMUE BROWN

ILLUSTRATIONS BY TOM BROWN

SNOWBOOKS

Proudly published by Snowbooks

Copyright © 2014 Professor Elemental, Brynneth Nimue Brown,
Thomas Sewall Brown

Snowbooks Ltd | email: info@snowbooks.com | www.snowbooks.com

British Library Cataloguing in Publication Data. A catalogue record for
this book is available from the British Library.

Ebook 9781909679191

Slipcase 9781909679276

Paperback 9781909679993

Letters Between Gentlemen being a selection of personal writings and correspondence, collected with much patience and diligence for your enlightenment. My aim as the editor of this collection was to clarify certain, now historical, events, and to shed light upon some of the greatest crimes and mysteries of our age.

At least, that was the theory, but frankly some of this stuff is a little far-fetched and suggests insobriety or worse. Also it is possible that some of the letters were written by women. It may be read therefore as a treatise upon the dangers of imbibing intoxicants. Although I fear readers will pick it up in search of wanton titillation and gratuitous gratification, to which end all images of exposed table legs have been carefully removed.

Wilberforce Wilfred Williams
The Editor

Dear Professor Elemental,

When you spoke of publicly endorsing our fine array of teas, we had no idea of the shame and ignominy you would bring upon our establishment. After due consideration, we, the Mapplethwait Tea Emporium, have a new proposition which we feel will be to our mutual benefit. We will undertake to make monthly payments to you for the rest of your natural life if you guarantee to stay away from our tea products in public places and cease suggesting that our tea is in any way suitable as a rocket fuel. The untimely deaths of several gentlemen of science, for which we hold you entirely responsible, have not created the public image of refined taste that we wish to cultivate.

Sincerely,
Fustram Mapplethwait

§

From the Diary of Algernon Spoon...

The people who come into my office are always guilty. Some are ashamed and need to make amends. Others wish to hide the evidence, pay off the victim, or make good their escape. Some have mysteries to solve, but rare is the person who sits down before me and speaks the unadorned truth. They all have something to hide. On odd occasions, there are just human weaknesses and minor failings they would prefer me not to know. I don't see a great many of those.

You won't have heard of me, I hope. It has been my earnest endeavour for the last three years to avoid all publicity. I do not court the papers, nor do I crave notoriety or public acclaim. Furthermore, my clients tend to be people who have no desire to see their misfortunes made public. Or their misdemeanours. These clients pay well for the work I do, for my silence and my co-operation. Before you jump to hasty conclusions about the ethical dimensions of my efforts, I shall say only this: There is a great deal of difference between criminality and impropriety, and I pride myself on being able to distinguish between the two.

We begin where all such tales of my profession must commence: with the woman who walks into my office and places some impossible, dangerous thing before me.

It was a grey, damp evening, of the variety London specialises in. I never have bright lights in my reception rooms; my clientele are invariably more at ease with the soothing camouflage of gloom. I do not need to see their faces plainly to assess them, but they do not know this. The tone of voice, the precise posture, the nervous fluttering of a hand. I read them all.

This filly was as cool as a cucumber sandwich. Long hair piled neatly on her head. Perfect skin, a swan's neck, and a

Algernon Spoon

SUSPECTS THIS WAS NOT PART OF THE ORIGINAL DESIGN

way of moving which suggested something about the precise journey her legs made from the ground upwards. This wasn't one of my abandoned wives, worried mothers, or vengeful former mistresses. She was a whole other class of being, and I knew straight away that it would be no run-of-the-mill case.

Her appearance was calculated to give an impression of neat, decorous gentility. But even in the low light of my office, her eyes told a different story.

"Good afternoon, Mr Spoon," she said. "I'm so glad you could see me at such short notice."

I gave her my hand and made all the usual soft, encouraging noises I produce for the first interview. I never ask difficult questions at the first round if I can help it. I wait until my services have been engaged and a deposit paid. It does not pay to make the guilty feel nervous, or to demand too much of a troubled conscience before the contract is signed. They panic all too easily.

Suitably encouraged, she settled down and began to tell her story. "It is a most difficult situation," she began.

I nodded sincerely, but of course they all say this.

"I fear I may be in danger, even coming here, but I must speak, or I fear something even more terrible will befall us."

She wrung her hands together like a woman in distress, eyelids lowered on those deceptive, gleaming orbs. I knew she was going to lie to me.

"I do not need to know the intimate details of your concerns at this stage," I reassured her. "Why not begin by explaining what it is that you think I might do for you. From there, I can ask questions only about that which may impinge upon the business, and you can take solace in saying no more than is strictly necessary. That might be more comfortable for you, yes?"

She looked up at me, dark eyelashes fluttering over her pale cheek. I watched a spot of colour bloom on her face, and wondered if she could do that deliberately. It looked to me like she'd be the very sort for such a charade. Still, I went through the motions of belief, ever the diligent employee.

"Murder is being committed," she said. "The police... oh, they are such ignorant fools, they haven't paid it the least attention. Death by misadventure, is all they say."

I nodded encouragingly. "Why do you not then tell them of your suspicions?"

She sighed. "I am afraid that if they do look closely, they will pick upon my poor, innocent brother."

That, at least, I had not heard before. "And why would they do that?"

"He has been used, terribly. It is a plot. And my poor brother is such a simpleton, so trusting and naïve, I believe he has been led on. I have tried to speak of my concerns to him, but my brother is an old-fashioned, country gentlemen, and he has certain beliefs about the place of women."

"You do not strike me as being a country mouse," I said casually, curious to see what she would make of this.

"I was sent away to be educated, and hope I am not too

dreadfully provincial any more." She smiled at me, pleased with herself.

No, she didn't seem to have a drop of provincial mud in her body. She was pristine city to the core, I felt certain. Or, at least, she'd been passing herself off as a sophisticate for long enough that it may as well have been her point of origin.

I decided I may as well cut to the chase. "Am I to understand, then, that you believe your brother is being framed for murder? The police do not consider the death suspicious, and your brother believes nothing is amiss."

"That is the essence of it, yes."

"At present, you and your family are in no immediate danger, by the sounds of it. Why risk public exposure and scrutiny? Why not let the matter pass by?"

She gasped. "Do you not think murder is immoral? Would you not act to stop such foul play?"

"I am engaged to assist people in resolving difficulties, and I do so within the boundaries of the law. However, my motivation is not a consideration here. It would be most helpful for me to understand why you wish to take this business forwards, against the advice of your brother and in opposition to the assessment already made by the police."

"There has been more than one murder," she said. "I do not know where it will stop. I fear for my brother's life. I fear for my own life, Mr Spoon."

"In which case, your concern is entirely understandable. Tell me, who benefits from these deaths?" I asked. The money usually provides the surest trail to the criminal.

"This is the most shocking part," she paused to draw a deep breath. "Thus far, Horatio and I have been the greatest beneficiaries. You can see how bad that looks for us."

"And you have a theory about who is framing your brother? And, I assume, some idea as to why this is occurring?"

"I have a theory, and a little evidence, but as for why… well, the letters speak for themselves. The man is clearly desperate for money and has already manipulated Horatio into parting with great sums. As Horatio's wealth increases, so too does his benevolence. There is also a matter of my own future; you will see I am right to be anxious, for the cad intends to marry me. By that means he will benefit from murdering my dear friends and relations." She dabbed her eyes with a delicately embroidered handkerchief.

It sounded like a most peculiar affair. "Do not distress yourself. I will take your case. I require some funds in advance, and I will report to you weekly at an address of your choosing."

"Might I come to you?" she asked. "I would not wish to risk a letter from you falling into the wrong hands. My life may be in danger."

"If you feel safer coming here then, by all means, do so. In the meantime, I will make what enquiries I can into your situation."

"Thank you." She dipped into her bag and removed a

bundle of papers. "You may find these helpful. My brother does not know that I have taken them, but he can be absent-minded and probably won't notice they're gone."

I accepted the letters with a polite murmur. "May I have a name? It makes it so much easier to plan meetings and arrange documents. It need not be your own name, just something we can use for our shared convenience."

She laughed a little at that. "The letters will reveal me, so I may as well be perfectly honest with you. My name is Miss Plunkett. Maude Plunkett."

"I shall endeavour to be of service to you, Miss Plunkett."

She thanked me and sashayed from the room. It had all the ingredients to draw a mind such as mine: the allure of death, the possibility of a real and complex plot, the hope of uncovering a villain.

I must observe that there are few pleasures in life that I relish more than killing a man in the line of duty, in the sure and certain knowledge that the law will commend me for my actions.

§

Dear Mr Mapplethwait,

Your last letter was a little confused. I'm sure all of the publicity I have brought to your fine teas must be a source of such joy that it entirely explains your incoherence. A monthly payment would be splendid. Please make arrangements with Hestons and Hestons, suppliers of matter for experiments in chemical and technical engineering. I'm sure they would be very pleased to receive money on my behalf and might then be persuaded to let me have some more saltpetre. I've been burning your tea for several days now, anticipating that it will make a fine charcoal substitute for use in small explosive devices. I plan a children's range for the next festive season. Ideal for youngsters with too many fingers. Let me know if you would like to see some samples.

As ever, it has been a pleasure to do business with you, sir.

Sincerely etc,
Professor Elemental

§

Dear Mister Hoghmes,

Thank you for leaving your calling card at the Private Detective Agency of Mister Algernon Spoon today. Mister Spoon regrets that he was unable to see you and asks me to convey that, while he was touched by your offer of a business partnership, it is his preference to work alone. Furthermore, you may want to consider that Mister Spoon favours discreet and unpublicised cases, while your approach has been notably high profile. The societally-visible modus operandi you have adopted would not suit him. He wishes you well and asks me to express his warmest respects to you.

Sincerely,
Alison Spoon
(Secretary)

§

From the Diary of Algernon Spoon...

The Plunkett letters had all most likely been written to the same chap – by the name of Professor Elemental – but it wasn't conclusive. At least, the handwriting bore similarity throughout. I noted radical variance in both the condition and the quality of paper. At times the hand was neat and easily read, while at others it rose and fell across the page, almost wave-like in its motion. I suspected at once that there might be liquor at work here. Although I am entirely free from such vices, I have a sense of their impact upon the lives of others.

I made several guesses at the running order, but there were no dates to guide me. Considering these letters alone, Miss Plunkett did indeed seem to have cause for concern. There were references to death and to herself. I think any normal maiden would tremble from one cause or another in reading such observations as I now held in my hand. However, I could see that without the counterpoint of the intervening

Alison Spoon with Bicycle
BEFORE THE NASTY BUSINESS WITH THE DEAD SHEEP

letters written by Mr Plunkett, I could not hope to assess the situation. Clearly there had been an exchange.

It did not take me a great many enquiries on the following day to find an advertisement for Professor Elemental's balloon flights, leaving London and carrying passengers to sunny Ipswich. I at once became suspicious of his character, for a man who touts a place like Ipswich as suitable for recreation is either a fool or a charlatan. I have been to Ipswich on only one occasion and found it wholly disagreeable. Once one has a taste for London life, it is hard to be quite at ease anywhere else. However, from the advertisement, I was able to procure an address. The simplest method seemed to be contact by letter. My job would be much easier if this Elemental fellow would co-operate quickly and release the Plunkett letters to me. How to persuade him? Flattery? Bribery? The truth?

Reading the character of a man is the essence of my work. These letters gave me an impression of one who might be either a genius or entirely detached from his right mind. He could be a vain fool or possessed of wisdom. The wrong move would impede the case considerably, while the correct pitch would, I felt sure, place the all important documents in my hands.

After some deliberation, I composed the following letter:

Dear Professor Elemental,

I feel certain you will not have heard of me, because I am

Travel to Ipswich

NO REFUND FOR FATALITIES

invariably overshadowed by the subjects with whom I work. My name is Algernon Spoon, and I present myself to you as one who wishes to do you a service.

Sensitive as I am to a man's need to keep the public at bay whilst holding up the profile necessary for public work, I approach you on a topic that I hope will be of interest.

As you are no doubt aware, publishing the private letters of public figures continues to be a popular way of making a living. I have in my hands a selection of your letters to one Horatio Plunkett, which I have been asked to print and make public. I never print private letters without first securing the permission of the author, and I always pay handsomely for such contributions. Reading your letters to this Plunkett fellow, I see what great pains you have gone to, explaining matters of science to the uninitiated layman. As the majority of our reading public will be no better informed than the good Mr Plunkett, I feel that we could increase the value of this project by printing his letters as well, so that the collection shows to best effect the progression of your exchange leading up to the now much talked about water-slide.

You cannot imagine my excitement at having such a cutting edge project and its letters come to my attention. It would be a great honour, sir, to put your work before a wider public. To this end, it would be a great help if you would furnish me with the other half, the lesser half, of this conversation so that your own words can be better framed and shown off, in all their wisdom and brilliance. If you are amenable to the project, I shall send a proper contract as soon as I have heard from you.

Your faithful servant,
Algernon Spoon

Editor's note: I should like to pause and make it clear that I no way endorse the underhand methods employed by Mr Spoon at this juncture. A collector should depend on the more honourable and accepted methods of our trade, namely going through bins, bribing servants and offering money to dissolute descendants of the great and the good. I have never deliberately lied to any of my sources. If I have misled anyone who has contributed material, to this, or any publication, it has been entirely by accident and a consequence of their imbibing far too much liquor. That I have on occasion been known to supply liquor is a wholly different issue, as the 'drunken' method of fact gathering is actively recommended by both the Little Red Police Handbook and The Nice Paisley-Covered Edition of Advice for Publishers and Collectors and is therefore a perfectly legitimate approach.

I have often found that, in the quest for truth, a great deal of deliberate dishonesty is often called for.

However, it would not be unreasonable to pause and recognise my own skill and cunning at this stage of the case, for my words hit their target precisely, and it was not long before this very pleasing letter found its way to my desk.

With it, all manner of things occurred to me. Before we go deeply into my thoughts, I shall share the letter so that you and I, dear reader, stand upon a more even footing.

Sir,

Thank you for your letter; it is a pleasure to receive correspondence from someone with a genuine interest in my work.

Well, if you know of me, then you know that I, too, shy away from publicity and cheap gimmicks to get attention. Certainly there have been times where my scientific discoveries have necessitated an audience, particularly the unveiling of the giant golden automotron that I unleashed in Norwich last year. (Yes, I had designed it to have my face and to bellow my words out at excruciating volume, and yes, I did unleash it on a busy shopping day – but this was really to prove a scientific point, rather than to gain attention. I forget what the scientific point was, but the giant golden robot professor certainly won't be forgotten by the people of Norwich any time soon. Particularly by those who lost loved ones in the tragic rampage that followed.)

So please do publish my letters. I only hope that they provide some inspiration for future water-slide builders or giant wasp-herders. And, of course, if you need any further information from me, please do not hesitate to get in touch (although ideally not in person. Geoffrey takes great offence

THE PROFESSOR TOOK PRIDE IN HIS SUBTLE CREATIONS,
SEEING THE ADVANTAGES OF STEALTH

to anyone arriving at the house unannounced. Or announced. Or any one at all, really).

Yours etc. etc. sincerely and so forth,
Professor Elemental

And so it was that Professor Elemental entered my life in a more immediate fashion. I did not allow myself too long enjoying the fruits of my own fine planning. There were serious questions to consider. Was the man as charming and naïve as his tone suggested? Or did I recognise here the strategy of a brilliant, but entirely evil and criminal mind? I could only wonder: was I luring him into a trap at that very moment, or had the bait been laid that would entangle me in a scheme too complex to imagine? Could I at last have found a nemesis equal to my own genius? Where lays the bluff?

I took the now-complete stack of letters back to my lodgings and settled down to put them in order. An almost coherent shape slowly emerged. When I was entirely confident that I had the right of it I set about reading them from beginning to end, so as to fully absorb their implications. Over tea and muffins, I considered each word carefully. But I get ahead of myself, and so we shall go slowly, you and I, into the mystery.

Here it begins, with a letter purporting to be written by one Mr Plunkett. But was it his work? Already I had suspicions.

§

Dear Sir,

I think it unlikely that you will remember me, but I wished to commence a correspondence with you because of the considerable impact your genius has had upon my life. We have not been properly introduced, but as we are clearly both gentlemen of good breeding, I trust that you will not take offence at my pushing myself upon you in this unusual manner. I am, quite simply, in awe of your genius and keen to learn more about your fabulous inventions.

We conversed briefly at the Marvels of Modern Science and Experimentation exhibition in Manchester about a year ago. I had the unrivalled delight of purchasing one of your antomatic devices and was able to observe a number of other wondrous creations before that most unfortunate scuffle occurred. I hope that you suffered no lasting damage? I had little choice but to depart from the affray. My general impression was that you work in a wide range of experimental fields, although I was not able to inspect any of your other devices as closely as I would have preferred.

My name is Horatio Plunkett, distantly connected to the Hampshire Plunketts, but not, I must confess, in any way related to the Irish Drax-Plunkett line. I have a small pile in Kent and a little place in Bath, but am not one for high society, so I doubt you will have heard anything much of me.

Part of my reason for writing is to pose what I fear may be a somewhat indelicate question. Due to the scuffle in Manchester, my purchasing of the antomatic was not accompanied by any instructions as to the purpose and best use of this fascinating object. Through my own judicious experimentation I have established, beyond all reasonable doubt, that its function has little to do with maiden aunts, or, I suspect, married ones, although the coroner was perfectly reasonable about the whole business and assured me it was the kind of mistake any chap could make. One of the consequences of the unexpected demise of my maiden aunt is that I find myself in possession of the means to further my own scientific interests. And, so, I apply to you, wondering if I might be allowed to view a few more of your creations and perhaps acquire a few for the collection I hope to build. I will not insult you by offering payment at this stage. I recognise that no money could truly compensate such genius as yours. However, vulgar though the topic of commerce is, I wish to assure you that I am a man of means and genuine in my interest.

Your most sincere and admiring servant

Horatio Plunkett

At this point I note the demise of a maiden aunt and the arrival of an inheritance. One could easily imagine the worst.

Sir,

Thank you for your recent communication. I apologise

Horatio Plunkett

POISED FOR ACTION, ADVENTURE, ROMANCE

OR A NICE AFTERNOON NAP

that I have not been in contact sooner, but some unfortunate business involving the Duchess of Kent and my team of racing chimps has delayed my progress in responding to letters of late*.

(* I should point out here that although the Duchess has since declared that she thought the chimps unsuitable for a garden party, she never specified that I *couldn't* bring them when she sent out the invitations. As for the unfortunate business that followed, well, I can hardly be blamed for the chimps' natural, inquisitive instincts.)

Of course I remember you, sir. I remember your keen attention to my inventions, your enthusiastic manner and garish waistcoat. Indeed, I remember you being so enthusiastic that you continued to talk long after the other guests at the demonstration had left! Indeed, if I were an unkind fellow, I might even suggest that you were the reason that they left so early. However, I am not unkind, so wouldn't dream of suggesting such a thing. No, indeed.

As for the 'technical difficulties' that I faced during the demonstration, I should point out that my machine did not malfunction and I was simply trying to show that all science comes with a price. Unfortunately for the chap in the front row, the price this time was the loss of a hand and the sight of his left eye. Still, what better opportunity to offer the services of my new automated limbs and telescope eye? The fellow in question was so stunned at my generous offer that he barely said a word. He is, of course, still unconscious in hospital, but

I rather think he will be 'over the moon' with the surprise of a pneumatic hand and a telescope in place of his left eye, when (and if) he wakes up.

I must confess that I am unfamiliar with your family line, although I myself have had piles in Bath and a small bath in Kent, so I am sure that our paths will have crossed at some point. So you acquired my machine in the end, sir? Congratulations are in order, then. It is hardly my business to explain its full purpose; after all, if you can't work that out, what business do you have in owning it! I should think it should be most obvious. I will say this, though: when you do turn it on, please ensure you have hot towels, a spanner and plenty of butter to ensure that it runs smoothly. Easy access to an emergency exit probably wouldn't go amiss, either.

As for payment, you are quite right: it is a vulgar business being paid for my nights and days of endless hard labour. What business does commerce have in matters of science? It is unnecessary to even consider such matters and I will be happy to furnish you with whatever you need… Of course, if you found yourself overburdened with monies, I would be only too happy to help you invest some or all of your fortune, purely to further the progress of science. How much did your aunt leave you, exactly?

I am keen to help however I can, sir; perhaps if you have a particular problem or requirement in mind for my machines, I can see if I can come up with something to 'fit the bill'. I have happily helped a great number of folk in a similar manner over the years and am yet to hear a single complaint, particularly as many are either hospitalised or unfortunately deceased.

I look forward to hearing from you,
at your earliest convenience,
Professor Elemental

Letter of uncertain date found amongst the Plunkett correspondence...

Dear Sir,

I am returning the entire consignment of goats which were delivered, dead and dying, to my estate. I spoke in jest when I said that, even for a hundred of the finest goats, I would not permit my daughter to speak with you, much less marry you. Two hundred mouldering goats do not constitute an engagement. Kindly never enter our county again.

Lord Edgbaston Troutwallop

Editor's note: While Mister Spoon came to this letter by accident, it pertains to a whole exchange which I include later for clarity. The Troutwallop letters go some way to illustrating the complex character of The Professor, and academic minds may wish to reflect on the reoccurring theme of goats and the impact of personal intimacy, or a lack thereof, upon the whole sorry business.

Dearest Professor,

I am ecstatic at receiving a letter in your very own handwriting, glorious and complex as it is. Nay, one might even go so far as to say that I am overwhelmed with jubilation. You cannot imagine my delight in hearing that you do indeed recall my humble self. I always say that if a man cannot lavish a little luxury upon himself in the waistcoat department, what point is there in even getting out of bed in the morning? I have received many compliments upon their bold and striking colours, but the style is all due to the excellence of my tailor. I cannot claim any natural gift for following fashion and am glad to have such an excellent chap at my disposal.

I return then to the business of my deceased aunt, and the antomatic. I fear that a semantic error may have inclined me to assume that the antomatic might be compatible with the maiden aunt, but I see now that butter would likely have made a lot of odds in the matter. Some blame for it all must be laid at the dear lady's door, although I do not like to speak ill of the dead. She read rather too many magazines for ladies, and had a morbid fascination with medical devices. It was with uncharacteristic enthusiasm that she took your innocent device to her private rooms, confident that she understood its purpose. A tragic mistake. One which, based on the observations of her doctor, I now realise could have been entirely averted had she only thought to use a little butter. As you observed so astutely yourself in your kind letter to me, science does indeed have a price and the ignorant meddle at their peril!

With reference to the Duchess of Kent, I have heard it said that she is not a forward thinking woman in either her choice of entertainments or her serving arrangements. I have even heard it said that she is an opponent of progress, which is a most damning accusation. This, one might almost say 'mediaeval', response to the charming novelty of chimps would serve as further indication of this in many more enlightened minds. Such as my own.

I understand that the recently formed Ancient Order of Hermetic and Scientific London Gentlemen ranks you as one of the most daring inventors of our time. Apparently your inventions have immobilised more people than Lord Heston's to date, and you are credited with more 'death by misadventure' cases than Dr Scwatch. I noted with interest that there are only seven professional gentlemen in all of Britain whom the Ancient Order deems to have been more dramatic in their efforts to advance science. I have no doubt that in due course you will top them all. To this end, I have enclosed a small sum to further the good work. I am still in the process of sorting out my late aunt's affairs, of which she turns out to have had a surprisingly large number. It may be a few months before my full inheritance is known, but in the meantime, I hope a hundred pounds is not too small a sum to enable the commencement of a modest research project? I leave the direction of the work entirely to you.

Might I enquire what kind of device you would recommend for a gentleman who favours the sporting life and is enthusiastic about shooting just about anything, but who suffers from unsteady hands and the decrease of eyesight inevitable with old age? I ask, not on my own account, but with regards to a dear friend and neighbour.

> Yours, with all the gentlemanly affection it may be considered appropriate to express,
> *Horatio Plunkett,*

Sir,

Thank you again for the kind words and the even kinder money. You may have read some unfortunate and rather disparaging stories about me in the London Times, regarding my losing a fortune in a silly bet about sending animals to the moon! Let me assure you, that, while there may be some truth in these stories, and that they may be entirely accurate, your money has been spent only on furthering scientific progress for the benefit of all mankind. And not just creating space-bound projectiles for donkeys. Not this time, anyway.

Your tailor sounds like an interesting chap, and rather familiar. I had some sort of an uncle who was in the tailoring trade for some years. He was, for all intents and purposes, as blind as a fruit bat on a sunny day, which was not only the reason for his retirement, but also puts me in mind of how someone might have allowed that waistcoat of yours to go on sale. I wonder if the two fellows are related?

My condolences regarding your aunt. She sounds like a woman of rare breeding and adventure. Too often, the fairer sex are timid, flimsy things, concerned only with needlework, idle chitter-chatter and horses. I have yet to find a woman who is brave enough to accompany me on my adventures, or indeed try many of my machines first-hand, despite my screaming of enthusiastic assurance. In fact, sometimes it feels like word has gone 'around town' that I am some sort of eccentric, as women often run away from me before I have had a chance to get to know them properly. Yes, I admit there have been three or four unfortunate incidents such as the one you describe with your aunt – but what is romance without the occasional adventure, experiment or broken limb? I am engaged in a lonely, lonely business, sometimes. Science can be a harsh mistress: at once vibrant and steamy and painful and unpredictably dangerous near an open flame. Much like my own departed mother, I suppose.

Forgive me, sir; you do not need to know the personal business of this particular professor. Let us return to more fitting matters, such as your forthcoming fortune. I hope that, by the time this letter reaches you, you have been able to establish the exact sum to which you are due and that you might be happy to share this figure with me, as your new friend, so that I might in turn share your burden a little. For indeed, wealth can be a burden if handled alone – I should know, I have lost more money than I have had hot dinners! (Particularly now that I can rarely afford hot dinners.)

What I propose is this, sir. You help govern the direction of my next invention (and indeed help with some minor funding issues) and I shall build the machine of your dreams. Want to travel to the centre of the Earth by water-slide? Need trousers that allow you to travel in time? Wish to speak to animals using a special hat? All of these things are entirely possible (or, at the very least, possibly probable); you guide me, sir, and I shall forge ahead, using the scythe of ingenuity to cleave a new path in the field of science! The mysterious but well-meaning Ancient Order of Hermetic and Scientific London Gentlemen are quite right: I shall soon top them all. Might I ask how you came to know about the Order? Although I have heard many whispers of their works, their meeting place and members are not easy to track down.

Oh, and regards to your neighbour who still enjoys an afternoon's shooting – tell him to carry on, and with gusto! The aforementioned uncle was an enthusiastic huntsman for many years, despite his lack of sight. Although his part in the hunt was unfortunately curtailed when he set his dogs upon Lord Wrexham (he had assumed that the fox had leapt upon His Lordship's head, when in fact Lord Wrexham was simply in possession of a full head of reddish hair) the thrill of the hunt kept him alive and vibrant in his latter years. Indeed, when no longer allowed to hunt foxes with dogs, he scaled down and trained guinea pigs to hunt voles around his living room. Sometimes he even tried to tie mice, dressed in full hunting gear, to the backs of the aforementioned guinea pigs, albeit with limited success.

So good luck to you, good luck to your decrepit neighbour and let's begin this endeavour together!

Sincerely,
Professor Elemental

P.S. Please do not mention that charlatan Lord Heston. His ridiculous ideas of telephonic communication and travel by horseless carriage are the stuff of fantasy and have no place in the realms of scientific progress.

My Dear Professor,

Next time you are in London, you must let me know, and I shall take you to dinner. We might be able to round up a few Hermetic and Scientific London Gentlemen to join us. I have no doubt that part of the confusion around our little enclave has to do with that unfortunate bunch of splitters, The Venerable Order of Hermetic Gentlemen. I had the pleasure of joining the original and far superior organisation a few months ago and am still rather too new to talk with much authority. It's all very jolly, though: all a chap could ask for in terms of secret signs, lengthy dinners and charming aprons!

We had a most excellent debate last week – one on which I should be delighted to hear your opinion. One of the chaps suggested that Borneo Spiggot should be considered for the listings, as he's reputed to have killed dozens of people. I suspect that you will no more have heard of the man than I had – he's one of those Northern industrial types, piles of money but no family name to speak of. And, of course, the deaths he has caused are all poor people, in his mills. There's barely any proper record of them. It doesn't seem quite on a scale with knocking off proper gentlemen through the pursuit of science! There is also the issue that he merely uses other men's ideas, rather than creating his own devices. The anti-Spiggot camp carried the day, to my considerable delight.

I have heard one or two things about the unmentionable Lord. He does seem very extravagant in his thinking, and really, I see little application for most of his schemes. I saw him, perhaps a month ago, waving around some kind of handset. He looked a little insane, clutching it to his head and muttering arcane anecdotes into its depths. I am sure some mention was made of talking to God, but, undoubtedly, the church is far more visually appealing if one must dabble in such things.

A device of my choosing, eh? I have restrained myself thus far, but delight overcomes me. I have enclosed a little more funding, just to be on the safe side. I am most intrigued by the water-slide. I recently invested in a most charming bathing suit, which seems fortuitous, if not an omen! Let it be the water-slide. If you do have any of the donkey firing devices left, I know just the man who would enjoy one. Do let me know, and I shall arrange for a cart to pick it up.

Where matters of the fairer sex are concerned, I can only comment that nature has blessed me with a number of sisters, and between them they have left me no less at sea than yourself. Maude's a good sort, with enough sense to get by, but the others are much as you describe – full of air, mirth and ringlets. I am doing all that a brother can to marry them off, but it is a tiresome business. If you would like one, I am sure we could come to some suitable agreement, but they are all rather silly. Aside from Maude – but she is not likely to wed, I think.

Yours in great excitement,
Horatio Plunkett

Sir,

Apologies for the delay in my writing to you. When attempting a small amount of 'do it oneself' around the house, I accidentally smashed through an interior wall and became trapped under a hefty wardrobe. Fortunately, Geoffrey was there to raise the alarm. Unfortunately, we must remember that he is an ape and incapable of even the most basic tasks. The well-meaning beast took my cries of pain and screams to 'send help' as simple requests for more bananas. There was, of course, no danger I would starve – but it still took over a week to free myself from the furniture which had become my nemesis and then to give Geoffrey the beating he so soundly deserved.

Why I keep him around is beyond me, sometimes.

So then, to business. Firstly, as your associate and, I hope to some degree, your friend, I feel I must warn you about your new-found colleagues at the Hermetic and Scientific club. I have heard whispers on the grapevine about shadowy dealings, underground chambers and worship of a most un-Christian kind*. (*Many of which rumours involved one or more goats.) I cannot prove any of these allegations, so I will go no further, only to say that the fellow who told me about it all was recently found dead. Hanging upside down. On a pentagram. In an underground chamber. Next to a dead goat, in a robe and a badge which read 'The Hermetic and Scientific Club'. Just to clarify, the goat was not wearing the robe, or, as I understand it, the badge. These things can be fearfully complicated, and I do like to have my facts straight.

Still, these sorts of accidents do happen, as my recent wardrobe adventure attests, and I am sure it is most likely simple coincidence. Still, if they offer for you to attend any 'midnight meetings', it may be best to politely decline.

On to more savoury topics. I have good news indeed. Having begun on your water-slide, I can tell you that it is

Geoffrey

WE MUST REMEMBER THAT HE IS AN APE

looking marvellous. Carved out of wood, then finely polished (so as to avoid splinters in one's most delicate areas), it stretches nearly a half-a-mile in length. Once completed, it will shoot you (via cannon) through the water past delicately painted murals of my adventures and face – all at speeds upwards of seventy-five miles per hour!

Sadly, despite your kind financing, we have hit a slight 'snag'. In my enthusiasm, I built from the ground up and now the water only flows upwards. This, as I am sure you are aware, is quite impossible, so I will require a considerable amount to make the slide adhere to the laws of physics once more. Once that is complete, we should be well on the way to giving you the aquatic adventure you deserve... You shall surely be envy of your friends, once you have a wooden water slide decorated with pictures of my face that stretches the length and breadth of your property! And to think they said my inventions would never be of any practical use!

I would like to see our savage 'cousins' in the North try something like this – the likes of Spiggot and co. are most likely too busy eating coal and marrying their own sisters to try anything so ambitious.

Speaking of marrying one's sister, I would be very grateful if you might allow me to take your sister to tea next Tuesday. Maude sounds a delight, and despite her being a woman, I am sure we could have some wonderful conversation. I would be only too happy to share the details of any meeting that you might set up between me and her, so that you can be sure my intentions are honourable. Just one thing though: why is she unlikely to marry? It's not because she was born a gentleman, is part of a Siamese twin or is imaginary, is it? It's just I have had those sort of problems with ladies before.

Yours, enthused, curious and thoroughly sick of bananas,
Professor Elemental

My Dear Professor!

I have read your letter a dozen times since it came and am so overwhelmed with such an unusual mix of sentiments that I barely knew how to begin. Then there was the small matter of needing to verify a few facts, and I too have been delayed, although in less dramatic a manner than you good self. I fear this will be a long letter, but I will do my level best to make it a cracker!

I am sorry to hear of your misfortune with the wall and the bananas. I have been told that they are a most pernicious fruit and that they cause unhealthy excitement in women. I can only imagine the unspeakable horrors you must have endured. It is a testament to your strength of will and formidable character that you were able to survive such a setback.

Oh, your words of my water-slide fill me with rapture. I long to see it! Might I come and visit, to gaze upon this wonder of physical impossibility? I almost think it may be too important to risk interference, that it should be displayed in all its current glory, while you have all the time and funding that you need to study the implications of your anti-gravity water creation. I have enclosed a cheque to make sure you can commence at once with whatever needs doing. In the meantime, while the great work continues, I wonder if you might spare me some small thing? Some old device that you have no time for and that a lesser mind such as myself could study and learn from? I should be most grateful.

Which brings me to a choice between two rather more delicate and tricky matters. I have pondered how to speak of these things to you, my good friend, for I would not want to mislead you in any way.

My sister, then. I can assure you that there is no shortage of chaps who would like to marry Maude. Obviously, being related, I can only think of her in a fraternal way, but I gather that her beauty does tend to excite the passions of others. I think it fairest to you both if I say that Maude is an independently-minded girl. She currently enjoys the attention of a number of affluent and very generous suitors. She enjoys their intention to a considerable degree, in fact to such a degree that I think it unlikely that she will relinquish her current course in favour of matrimony. At least, not until age has accounted for beauty to some extent. I hope that you catch my meaning here, for I do not think I can say it more plainly.

As for the Hermetic and Scientific club, I have made a few tentative enquiries. I think it entirely possible that the unfortunate event you referred to was not in fact connected to the Ancient Order of Hermetic and Scientific London Gentlemen at all, but has instead been ascribed to The Order of Most Ancient and Hermitic Scientific Gentlemen of London. In most regards they exist purely to spite us, but I fear they have become carried away to an inappropriate degree with their nasty occultish meddling. The deliberate choice of a similar name results in both of our clubs being referred to casually as 'Hermetic and Scientific Gentlemen' or similar. It is most frustrating. At last month's celebratory session we were just opening the seventh bottle of finest whiskey when some fool insisted on trying to deliver a goat. We of course had not ordered a goat, and as it was still alive, we couldn't even persuade the cook to roast it for us. A mere half an hour later an irate chap arrived demanding the goat back, having delivered it to the wrong club. I ask you! The quality of working men in London is not what it should be.

Of the goat-bothering Gentlemen, I could believe almost anything. They have caused us a good deal of trouble, our own members being embarrassingly treated at a number of good establishments thanks to the confusion it has called. I had felt sure it is a plot to bring us into disrepute, but in light of this most unpleasant scenario with the deceased fellow, I hardly dare imagine what they are intending or where they might stop.

Rest assured, my dear friend, that the only invitations I accept in London involve dining at good houses. It would take a great deal to persuade me into any underground scenario. Wine cellars are for butlers, in my book!

I cannot tempt you to consider one of the other sisters, then? Matilda is quite pretty and plays the piano rather well, Catherine dances charmingly, but I'm afraid neither has much thought inside their pretty little heads, so perhaps it is as well. I cannot imagine you would have much use for a foolish wife. I shall probably find them suitable army chaps and get them bundled off to India; I am certain it would do them both the power of good.

I await the coming of your next letter with great enthusiasm. Please, please do send me a little device I can entertain myself with, and I shall promise faithfully to remain in the countryside with it and court no dangers at all amongst the shady folk of London. At least for a while.

Your friend,
Horatio Plunkett

Sir,

Forgive me, I write to you with some urgency as I am in somewhat of a predicament. There are no less than ten wasps the size of large house-cats roaming free in the manor and currently seeking my whereabouts. Ironically enough I have taken refuge in the self same wardrobe that I was previously trapped under, in the hope that these giant wasp bastards might choose another queen and leave me be.

I must, of course, take some of the responsibility for being at the mercy of giant wasps, as I did breed them under quite unnatural circumstance and then set them free in my home. It seems that my theory that 'wasps would likely begin creating super sweet wasp honey, if bred to giant size' was incorrect. It also seems that the London Scientific society's hypothesis that 'giant wasps would be ridiculous and bloody dangerous' was quite, quite true. Blast. I hate being wrong.

So then, I must be brief. As for the Hermetic and Scientific club, well, I shall take your word for it. I have often been mistaken for a 'mad' professor or an incapable gadabout, instead of the respected member of the scientific community that I clearly am, so I do understand the pain of being wrongly identified. Perhaps I might meet some of these chaps myself when I am next in London?

As for your sisters, Matilda and Catherine are perfectly adequate, I'm sure. If one simply needed to have someone squeeze out some children and sing songs about horses, I have no doubt they would be 'fit for the task'. However, Maude sounds right up my long, tree-lined path. I am not worried one jot about her 'other suitors'. One afternoon with me, and she would most likely forget all about them. And if she didn't, well, Geoffrey could always be tasked with speaking to them individually, so as to help them change their minds. By 'speaking', I do of course mean 'screaming and throwing things', as is the way of the ape. Might I be able to meet Maude in person, say, next Monday at Crumbling's Tea Parlour on Hodge Street, in the city? Perhaps at four?

Thank you for the funds. I am pleased to announce that the slide should be ready by Tuesday, whereupon we will have to make arrangements for it to be moved to your abode. It really is quite the thing and should satisfy your every need. Well, your every need to fly down a water-slide at a break-neck pace, anyway.

Oh yes, your gift. Well, I would have sent you a wasp, if they had proved better pets, but, as it is, they are best left well alone. Please take this small cube, instead. It may only be the size of a small tea pot, but this cube contains wonders. Think of it as a kind of 'Swiss Army cube'. As you can see it is lined with dark orange buttons, each one with a slightly different purpose and outcome. One might produce a hand which will give you a firm back rub, another button might produce a spring-loaded knife with which one can cut a potato or stab an intruder. One button will pop out a thermometer to test the temperature of a bath or cup of tea, the other will produce a small rotor with a powerful enough rotation to aid flight to up to one human man. Just don't press the red button, or you will doom us all.

Damn and blast it all, I must go, sir, I think they have

Super Sweet Wasp Honey

heard me dictating this letter to Geoffrey (he is in here with me, too) and are trying to open the door to the wardrobe with their mandibles.

Yours in mortal terror,
Professor Elemental

My Dear Professor,

I hope this letter finds you safely spared from waspish torment.

I have conveyed your wishes to Maude – she is not the sort of sister one can instruct, and she is of the opinion that she would like to meet you as proposed. Maude has never been one to accept the presence of a chaperone, and so will appear at the appointed time alone. In order to render herself recognisable, she will have a pair of flying goggles somewhere about her person. Dear Maude tends to have quite a turnover in suitors, not least because of her persistent disinterest in marrying any of them, so the deployment of this Geoffrey chap may prove complicated. However, there was an army fellow called Henry Goddingford who kept calling the other chaps out and shooting them. I think he's off to the colonies, which should put an end to that, but it's only fair to warn you. He's a little unstable, I fear.

Ah, the Swiss Army cube is a marvel. It kept us cheerfully employed for hours. We have already discovered that if you apply a long stick, or for that matter, a servant, the risks are much reduced. It does make the most charming noises. Even when we don't believe it's doing anything, it still produces sounds. Fascinating! Two of Catherine's kittens have gone missing since the cube arrived, but I don't think she's noticed yet. You are right, sir; I could not in all conscience wish Catherine or Matilda upon you. They are dear, sweet girls and will no doubt provide excellent mothers for the right sort of chap who wants a big family and will be a pleasing ornament for his parlour. At least, if they can be persuaded to take off their veils. They are slaves to this peculiar fashion, even about the house. I can't say I approve but I try to be a modern man and allow them to dress as they please.

It is almost uncanny that you fixed upon the idea of songs about horses. As I write this I can hear Matilda at the piano, her dulcet tones raised up in that patriotic classic, "The French Shall Not Eat My Darling Horse."

Should we, do you think, undertake to move the slide in one piece? Or might it be better to dismantle and re-construct it? I would not want any delicate parts to suffer the rude hardships of travel. I shall arrange a garden party once it is in place, and I shall beseech you to attend as my guest of honour. I am so full of intellectual excitement at this prospect that I can barely contain myself.

And yes, we must dine in London, with a few of the chaps.

There's nothing like a twelve-course dinner to stimulate good debate, I find. It would be an honour to be able to introduce you.

Your enthusiastic servant,
Horatio Plunkett

P.S., a little additional funding enclosed, to help with the considerations of moving the slide.

Sir,

Well, it's all turned out rather well in the end, hasn't it? By now I imagine that your slide has arrived and is in place around your home. No doubt you have already tried it and found it to your satisfaction – I can almost hear the screams of pleasure from here.

The wasps are gone. To be honest, I have no idea where. There were reports of a fête in the neighbouring village being beset with oversized *Vespula vulgaris*, but this is surely a coincidence. Either way, with a death toll of thirteen and several livestock reportedly carried away, it's best that I remain quiet on the matter for fear of unjustified reprisals.

So, as you sit in your slide and I enjoy sitting anywhere that isn't the inside of a wardrobe with an ape in a suit, perhaps it is time to turn to matters of the heart. Tomorrow I shall meet your sister. I look forward to getting to know her and seeing

Two Modest and Charming Sisters
AT HOME TO VISITORS ON TUESDAYS

her goggles, so to speak. I shan't bring Geoffrey; he is not great at first impressions and he has a meeting himself. (Well, I say 'meeting': he likes to gather the various animals on the estate and shout unintelligible noises at them. They often get quite 'riled up' and put me in mind of the revolutionary rabble I have seen in the colonies. Nonsense, of course, it is just a group of animals making noises and fashioning simple weapons out of household objects. Why not let them have their fun, I say – what harm could come from it!)

I look forward to meeting Maude and will bring a special poem writ just for the occasion. I shall wear my special trousers too. You might want to tell this Goddingford chap to stay well clear, though; I may be wearing my love trousers, but I shall have on my fighting socks just in case.

I shall let you know how I get on tomorrow. In the meantime, it may be best to leave the cube well alone. It is most likely safe now that it is full, but one can never be too careful.

Yours in anticipation of great romance,
Professor Elemental

PS. I should add that while Matilda is perhaps not the lady for me, I do admire her taste in melody and song choice. When we were young, dear Nanny used to teach us the following rhyme which is as true today as it was then:

'Damn the French! Please stay away!

I shall never let my horse stray,
For if a French man hides in hay
He will eat my horse today!'

Many's the time that she would warn us that, if we didn't sleep, the French would come and smear garlic over our innocent faces. It never happened, thankfully, but we always fell into a deep sleep just in case.

Dear Professor,

I send this little note to accompany a gift from my younger sister, Maude, who is most excited about meeting you. I suspect the gift will arrive after your meeting, but who knows? I shall encourage the messenger with coin of the realm.

Last year, Maude was examined by Albertus Pumpernickle, a Germany phrenologist we met whilst holidaying in Europe. He assured us that, as is usually the case with women, my sister has far too small and restricted a brain to be able to contemplate the rigours of science without serious risk to her health. Since then she has devoted herself to the gentler arts of vivisection and taxidermy.

It is our shared hope that you will enjoy this little selection of stuffed amphibians, arranged with tiny replica musical instruments.

Maude is a great admirer of your work in her own, small

way and was coincidentally the sole beneficiary of the estate of the lately-departed Sir Jeremiah Trumpet-Smythe. The unfortunate gentlemen died of shock in circumstances that remain unclear. I am sure it is a coincidence that I had loaned to him your most wondrous cube.

At present the water-slide is in the process of being properly assembled. I even went so far as to bang in a nail myself! But this is the extent of my empathy for the working man. They are going very slowly, damn them! Still, I have a list of guests drawn up for my garden fête, and there is much clamouring to be first to try out this modern wonder. I shall report to you as to the success of this, unless you prefer to come along yourself for the great day?

Sincerely yours,
Horatio Plunkett

Sir,

How kind of you to invite me to your home. Usually, if I am invited to come along and witness an invention that I myself have made, I prefer to keep my distance, for reasons of personal safety and in case of any complaint that may arise, in the unlikely incidence of the invention not quite working out as planned. Ever since my gift to the royal family of Belgium ended in such tragic circumstances, I have found that a little distance between me and my creations is well worth while.

(I am sure the King of Belgium would agree, if they weren't still scraping bits of him from the upper enclaves of St Paul's Cathedral.)

Either way, it is a testament to my confidence in this invention, and my assuredness that you are both friend and colleague in this endeavour, that I would be more than happy to meet. Might I bring Geoffrey? He is so rarely allowed off the property and promises to be on his best behaviour. I am reminded that it was he who accidentally reversed the mechanisms on the day of that tragic royal visit, but I will keep him close by, well-caged and out of his head on high-grade opiates.

The tiny lizards are a thing of beauty. Wonderful little fellows all, and they bring such whimsy to the manor. Certainly they have eyes that 'follow you around the room', and I am sure I saw one twitch slightly yesterday. But it may just have been a trick of the light, my failing eye sight or a gin-induced hallucination, (which have been increasing with alarming regularity since I began my 'all gin diet' some weeks ago in an attempt to rid myself of unwanted flab).

Alas, I waited and waited for dear Maude, but there must have been some mix-up. I did spend a most agreeable afternoon with a young lady who I met, believing it to be dear Maude, but it turned out after several hours that this particular lady's name was Dennis and that she was not a lady, but rather a foppishly-dressed fellow of an effeminate nature who rather took advantage of my keenness to impress and lavish tea cakes and buns on my date. Please send my most sincere apologies. Might I meet dear Maude at your home when I come and visit? Will she forgive me?

Sincerely and hopeful,
Your friend Professor Elemental

PS. Thank you for the monies that you sent with your message. The messenger himself was, to be fair, a half-wit who would likely have spent it on cheap ales, so, to save him from himself, I took the monies to buy gin with. I think it was the only kind thing to do.

My Dear Professor,

I must begin with most profound apologies on behalf of my sister. It was all due to the dreadful Goddingford, who is a plague. I am sure the Biblical plagues had nothing to compare to him. The man eats in a way I am sure locusts would be proud of and drinks in a manner that, quite frankly, betrays his Scottish ancestry. I have never approved of him. Unfortunately he responds to disapproval with death threats.

He kidnapped dear Maude on the very morning you were to meet. It's not the first time, but as she invariably escapes after a couple of days, the police never take an interest. Ah, if you had some small, lightweight and highly poisonous thing that a lady might carry... but no, I fantasise, and I would never dream of involving you in a murderous plot, no matter how vile and deserving the intended victim might be. Maude is safely returned to us now, but it may be a day or two before her usual, cheerful spirits return. Goddingford always has this deleterious effect on her sweet nature.

It is curious that you mention diets. I have not tried the gin diet. I have currently undertaken, as a bet with the Scientific and Hermetic chaps, to eat my way through the alphabet. We were talking a few days ago about how, with the great abundance of food types now available, a man can eat a different thing every day if he wants. Somehow from here we came to the idea of the alphabet challenge. Each day, only food beginning with a certain letter. I started well, with anchovies, apples, apple pie, apple crumble, artichokes and asparagus, almonds and so forth. My second day was a joy, bread, beer – mostly beer, in fact. Then cheese, cream, custard, cod – not all on the same plate! I have since come to question the wisdom of the scheme. Today I have eaten only ice cream. Tomorrow I cannot think of a single thing aside from jam, and a fellow cannot live by jam alone. Then kippers, kedgeree, and kale? The prospect alarms me. Lard and lupins perhaps…. And I am already pondering how to procure a zebra, because I cannot think of another remotely edible thing beginning with 'Z'. I suppose you don't know any zoological fellows who might sell me such a creature? This particular approach to eating does not appear to cause weight loss of any kind, but it does give the cook the most tremendously entertaining run-around.

Do, do come for the grand slide opening. My great uncle Harold has persuaded me that, despite his being about ninety, he should have the joy of descending the slide first. It will do his old heart good to be the centre of such joyful attention, I rather imagine. And do, do bring the delightful Geoffrey. I shall welcome him with open arms. Metaphorically speaking.

Ah, so many plans to make, so much excitement. I shall be on 'S' by the great day. I anticipate there will be salmon swordfish, shallots and sultanas on the menu, at the very least. Soufflé? It may not complement the gin diet entirely. Do they not put berries in gin? I had heard that berries are supposed to be beneficial to one's digestive tract, so that is no doubt the essence of the system.

Ah, the King of Belgium. I hadn't thought of him in, well, quite some time now. Would that all monarchs had such an adventurous spirit as he.

Your trusting friend,
Horatio

Sir,

I am sorry to hear of such tragedy in regards to your sister. This filthy Scottish cur sounds less a gentleman and more dirty dog. Possibly a one-eyed, mangy dog with fleas and gammy tail. One that isn't even a dog, but a rabid fox, a stupid, stupid, hateful fox. But I digress. I am of course quite outraged that my future love could be jeopardized by such a fiend. I haven't known intimacy since that unfortunate incident with Lady Flora Hastings and to a lesser extent, Sir John Conroy. And the less said about that the better. I shall not have true love snatched away by Scottish claws.

Enclosed is a small device – it looks like a perfume spray, and is small and compact. In fact, it was intended to be a new perfume, but after a brief and disastrous launch, 'Eau de Professor: The Stench of Invention' was shown to be a much more efficient poison than it ever was a fragrance.

One spray of my lead-based perfume will knock a bull elephant to its knees. Two sprays and that same elephant would be quite dead, but with a lingering, subtle aroma of elderberry, rosewater and lead. I only urge caution. I would hate for my gift to lead to some unforeseen tragedy – still, what are the chances of that!

In regard to matters of diet, I highly recommend that you steer clear of the all-gin diet. While no one could deny that I did lose a little weight, no one could also deny that I was eventually found naked and drunk in the National Gallery, shouting at a portrait of the Duke of Wellington that it owed me money. I had already had a brief scuffle with a statue of the Queen, and I do fear that I came off the worse from the whole encounter.

Your alphabet diet is much more the ticket. Let us arrange to meet on the day you are working through the letter Q.

The Stench of Invention

That way we can dine on quails and quince, and I will finally get to put my runcible spoon to practical use.

I remain at your disposal: please contact me if there is anything that I can do to aid this situation and place your sister back into my heroic, yet curiously thin, arms.

Professor Elemental

§

From the Diary of Algernon Spoon...

And finally this item of correspondence, which may or may not be related to the case...

You do not know me, but I come to all your talks, and I sit at the back and gaze at your lovely, lovely face. I am just a silly thing and do not understand half of the clever words you use, but I am enchanted by the manly grace of your knees, and when I think about you, I touch my own knees and pretend they are yours.

I want you to be mine forever. Please be my friend, my special, special friend. My other, much less special friends all call me Winny, which is short for Winifred, and has very little to do with my looking like a horse. I am yours forever.

I must have read the letters a dozen times, sitting up all the way through the night, much to the chagrin of my landlady, who does not approve of such wasteful living. My honesty with you, my dear, imaginary reader, may come as some surprise. I am aware that certain fashionable gentlemen who write up their society crimes inflate their importance through the means of literary games. The pre-meditated withholding of information enables them to seem that little bit smarter when the plot is finally revealed. I am indulging in no such tricks for self-aggrandizement. I have written my thoughts only as the case has unfolded so far, and I will continue to do so. I do not think that we will need any such machinations here. So often, when one lays the plot out in the linear way in which it must have first appeared, the mystery is not so complex after all. Hoodwinking the humble reader is not a mark of genius. I rather imagine that when I am weary of work and inclined to retire, these words will make the basis of some fine publication. Or else I shall leave them to posterity and avoid the limelight entirely. I have not yet decided.

And so, having considered the letters, I observe that one maiden aunt has clearly died due to an incident with an invention of Professor Elemental's. I also note one unnamed gentleman profoundly injured, the unspecified death of the Professor's own mother, the death of Sir Jeremiah Trumpet-Smythe and a definite risk to a gentlemen only identified so far as 'Great Uncle Harold'. Miss Plunkett's description of the case leads me to think that her concerns pertain to the death of Trumpet-Smythe and perhaps also the maiden aunt, and not to the other deaths alluded to. Still, considered as a whole, these letters present a curious picture, and one highly suggesting that deliberate murder for money has occurred, rather than the more innocent accidents of normal life to which these deaths have otherwise been ascribed. Motives and opportunities are clearly visible, but whose hand guides the plan? Which of these gentlemen is feigning the fool's role for his own evil means? Or should we look further afield, to the three sisters, Goddingford or some as yet un-named individual? It is a deep mystery.

§

Mister Hoghmes,

Thank you for the flowers, a most generous gesture on your part. Mister Spoon regrets that he was elsewhere today and unable to see you. He remains steadfast in his view that you and he would not make appropriate business associates. I trust that this now settles the matter.

Sincerely,
Alison Spoon (Secretary)

§

Lord Edgbaston Troutwallop (I decline to write 'dear' because you are anything but dear to me, so please do consider this an act of deliberate rudeness on my part. I should hate to think that your innate stupidity might cause you to miss the more subtle aspects of my mockery.)

Uncannily, your darling daughter said much the same thing to me about the goats, but it would be ungentlemanly of me to allude to the precise and intimate circumstances in which that exchange took place. The consequences of refusing my offer must be yours to bear, sir. I have given you fair warning and cannot be held responsible. Appolina will have to keep her burdensome fortune, and you will have no one to blame but yourself.

Professor Elemental

§

Mr Elemental (And no, you are neither dear, nor professorial in my book, and I am far too refined to even allude to your lack of manners),

How dare you even suggest that Appolina has entered your uncouth presence, much less imply intimate, nay Biblical, knowledge of her chaste and virtuous self? I have a good mind to shoot you.

Lord Edgbaston Troutwallop,
Five-times winner of the Surrey cup for marksmanship with both regular and improvised weaponry.

§

Lord Troutwallop,

Does your daughter not have a fine head of coppery hair, excellent teeth, pert buttocks and a considerable appetite for gin?

Professor Elemental,
Inventor of the steam-gun, the hand-held exploding perfume bottle and a lot of very pointy things, some of which also blow up unexpectedly.

§

Professor Elemental,

That sounds amusingly like my former butler, fired for appearing before guests in a dress. I'm so entertained by this thought that I shall refrain from shooting you so as to better enjoy your discomfort and public humiliation. This will make a most excellent anecdote for every party I attend during the rest of my life.

Lord Troutwallop

§

Lord Troutwallop,

On reflection, the moustache should have given me pause for thought, but aside from the mouldering goat issue, which I hope you will overlook as I now have all the goats anyway, I feel we may part as friends and never speak of this matter again.

Professor Elemental

§

From the Diary of Algernon Spoon…

Today I finished the case of The Sinister Knocking Sound. I dislike anything that smacks of the gothic or melodramatic, and would normally send away clients whose imaginations are troubled by reading too much fiction, or who are more generally unhinged by lack of proper usage of the brain. However, Abraham Stoppit's geographical location intrigued me. The antiquity of the house suggested connections to papist plots of ages past. My study of old maps led me today to uncover no fewer than three secret passages, currently frequented by criminal elements and used, it would appear, for storing smuggled goods. The appropriate authorities have been informed, my client has been rewarded, I have been paid and several good working men of London are now hissing through their teeth over the challenges of blocking said tunnels and whether it would be better for Mr Stoppit to keep them open in case of a zombie apocalypse.

I am now free to focus my intellectual powers on the Plunkett case, which I have yet to properly title, being unsure of whether a crime has even occurred, much less who should be blamed. Having had time to reflect upon the letters, I find there are certain other points that have attracted my attention. So many loose ends. So many possibilities. Perhaps Miss Plunkett is unaware of the recent hermetic murders in London. While there is no obvious connection between either Plunkett or Elemental and this case, I am alert to the possibilities.

I took a little wander into a more fashionable area and enquired amongst various acquaintances who work for the many gentlemen's clubs. They are, for the greater part, a discreet bunch, but I have found that broad, general questions that cannot incriminate any specific gentleman, and which are accompanied by a little ready cash, tend to be fruitful. Gentlemen in their cups can be most communicative, and it only takes the slenderest of threads to take an investigation forwards.

I found Lilly Godiva at The Whistling Pig, and, after a lengthy conversation about her mother's health, was able to establish that there is indeed an Order of Hermetic and Scientific London Gentlemen meeting regularly at Pinners.

"Rich boys tip well," she said with a smile.

"I suppose they must have very dull meetings," I suggested.

"Oh, no, they're a lot of fun, the Order," she said. "Lots of drinking and placing bets and daring each other. Proper gentleman's club, they are, and no mistaking. None of your clever stuff."

I made a few additional enquiries and confirmed that this little assembly did indeed seem to be quite harmless, and equally incapable of both Science and Hermeticism. I wondered why the papers had not commented on this interesting detail when reporting the recent murders. But then, sensationalism sells, and yet another drinking and gambling club does not. It does, however, make me wonder why these murders are occurring. There must be some connection between the Order and the nearly identically-named and far more shady outfits of similar title. Is one a cover for another? Is one a means for attacking some personage within another? Are the names merely cover for some wholly different murder motive? I am not certain this is even my case. It may be connected, it may not.

§

Professor Elemental. Note to Self.

Some kind of recording device on which notes to self can be kept safe from animals, experiments, fire, flood, giant wasps etc. etc. Train Geoffrey in shorthand? Hire someone to write things down? Find alternate method of payment that does not involve money in order to hire someone to write things down… this starts to sound horribly complicated. I can't be the only chap who cannot afford to hire a chap to make notes. Therefore, a device for this purpose is bound to attract money and thus fund the hiring of a suitable note-taker. Or I could blow it all on gin. Again.

Recording sound. Wax cylinders too short, too heavy, too prone to melting and something has chewed one of them. Whose silly ideas were these, then? To lock sound into a solid object, well, that worked nicely in my robot, but I only had a short speech, not a selection of fabulous ideas needing to be taken down in the moment. Geoffrey is no good, laughs far too often. What about parrots? How much can they remember and repeat back?

§

Plunkett Case Notes

The Order of Hermetic and Scientific London Gentlemen is simply an eating and gambling concern that likes to place bets on which notorious scientist, industrialist or similar gentleman will inadvertently kill the most people that month. A harmless enough distraction for wealthy idiots, which may explain a great deal about Mr Plunkett, or may be an elaborate cover for more nefarious activities. Other groups with similar names prove harder to locate, but I have ascertained that Plunkett is in fact a member of the gambling set and nothing more sinister – assuming the Order is indeed all it appears to be. A study of the membership list reveals a plethora of wealthy fools, industrialists who wish to associate with the upper classes and all the usual suspects for activities best ignored. Incest, debt, corruption, nepotism, and bagpipe playing – the normal gentleman's vices, in fact.

However, Plunkett has bet heavily on the success of Elemental when it comes to causing death. Is that a motive? How far will these gentlemen go to win their bets? Who are their friends? Will they push for greater risks to ensure a higher death toll? Is that even illegal? Would it be a reason for some other group to wish them ill? Ah, the evil that people undertake for money, and, for that matter, the unhelpful things people do in the name of innocent entertainment. Would that it were easier to tell them apart.

§

Mister Hoghmes,

Thank you for your kind gift of cakes. While your generosity is touching, Mister Spoon regrets than he cannot do business with you at this time.

Sincerely,
Alison Spoon

§

Professor Elemental. Note to self:

Parrots have worse memories than you do, Professor. Do not repeat your best plan ever to one, ever again. It was something involving badgers, I feel certain. Lovely badgers. Wouldn't they look good in maid's uniforms? The black and white, the paws.

Additional note to self: Invent perfume able to mask the

smell of badger. On a badger. If it were wearing a uniform. On a hot day. In front of the Queen.

Note to self: Talking to badgers mostly causes them to run away. What if the printing process itself could be sped up? Letters printed at the speed of speech! I need something that can hold the letters and push them down at the right moment. Mice have small hands. I have plenty of mice around the place. There is a whiff of genius about this. Whiff of Genius… that would be a good perfume name. Invent more perfume. Ladies like perfume. Party invitations. Nothing to wear. Get another black eye. Mmm. Note to self, do not invent any more perfume.

§

From the case notes of Algernon Spoon…

I have no doubt that money changed hands. Elemental is certainly keen to extract lucre, but in this he differs not one whit from a great many other enterprising gentlemen. I am more curious about the sheer enthusiasm of Plunkett to hand over cash. It is possible of course that I have witnessed the amusing clash of two crooked individuals, each keen to take terrible advantage of the other. And yet, that seems a little too simplistic, and I think there may be more to consider here. Again I ask, is gambling at the root of this? I am not convinced the money is a motive. What, then?

Having re-read these letters, I feel no doubt that the writer (who for now we shall assume is indeed Horatio Plunkett) considers Maude Plunkett to be a woman of dubious moral character. My own observations tend to support the notion. Was she Trumpet-Smythe's mistress? And what of this Goddingford fellow? I find myself with more questions than answers at present, but this is a most delightful discovery.

I shall settle down at once to compose another letter.

Dear Professor Elemental,

My thanks for your assistance so far. Can I enquire as to whether the garden party and water-slide launch took place? Did you attend the event? Your thoughts on this would be the perfect way to end the folio.

Sincerely,
Algernon Spoon

§

Mister Hoghmes,

I am returning the diamond ring, as I feel it would be too compromising for me to accept such a lavish and unwarranted gift.

When Mister Spoon says that he 'regrets' not being able to

see you, he is trying to be polite in rejecting your advances. He has absolutely no desire to see you and regrets not seeing you in the sense of really wishing you would go away and leave him alone. I hope this is sufficiently clear. Please do not send any further gifts or letters to either of us, at all, ever.

Thank you.

Sincerely,
Alison Spoon

§

From the Diary of Algernon Spoon…

Today I finally concluded the Widows and Orphans Friendly Society case, which I wish I had recorded in detail from the outset. It turned out to be so very much more interesting than I dared first imagine. My client, who, for the sake of anonymity we shall call Mr Owlnose, was entirely happy with my efforts. I call him Mr Owlnose due to a curious biological feature. I assume his nasal passages must frequently be blocked. When the good gentleman inhales, there is often a faint hooting sound accompanying the process. It is rather reminiscent of the barn owl, to be precise.

Mr Owlnose came to me some months ago, concerned that his only son had joined a Friendly Society for Widows and Orphans. A letter had been intercepted by the suspicious father who felt understandably uneasy about this development. I shall not name him, for he is a public figure, and he has paid me well to keep silent. There is no love lost between Owlnose senior and son of Owlnose: that much was obvious from the first. Son of Owlnose is a wastrel, a gambler and fond of keeping fast company. A young man likely to embarrass the father. Could he not be making amends now? I enquired. Might not the Widows and Orphans represent an inclination to do good in the world? After all, benevolence and charity are suggested by membership of such a group.

Mr Owlnose was having none of it. I took the simplest route and applied to join the organisation myself. They asked who had recommended me to them, not my condition or intentions, and my membership was barred. As this seemed a little peculiar, I delved deeper. There are so many orders and societies that restrict membership for the purposes of seeming important, after all, but my curiosity was aroused. Furthermore, Mr Owlnose was paying handsomely, and I never stint on checking details for affluent clients.

An organisation of any size leaves marks upon the world. It utilises rooms, sends letters, collects subscriptions. Tracking down such details is the slow and often tedious work for which I am employed. I have a mind for intricacies and no aversion to poking within the dustbins of those I am set upon. I am equally willing to listen at doors and spy through windows. I excel in matters of disguise, however. Once I had learned where meetings take place, I took the simple expedient of bribing a servant to swap with me, letting me wait at table for the evening. Having used such tricks before, I am entirely capable of carrying off the act. It has frequently been my experience that the wealthy do not quite perceive servants as being actual people. As a consequence, they reveal themselves.

The first session I attended gave me some half a dozen names to explore. Only half of them appeared to be either widowed or orphaned. On closer scrutiny, I found the other half had the potential to be heirs and heiresses of the future. Poverty did not feature in any of their lives. Yesterday I once again donned the apparel of servitude and presented myself as cup bearer to the Widows and Orphans Friendly Society. They were celebrating the success of a certain young man who had only that week achieved orphan status. From the tone it was evident that no grief had entered his youthful breast. He thanked the assembled people for their support, advice and encouragement.

Today I was able to confirm to Mr Owlnose that his fears were entirely founded. He has changed his will accordingly, making a nephew his sole inheritor. I now have a list of other gentlemen who are at considerable risk of accident or misadventure. Now to decide: is it a matter for the police? I am not convinced I have enough evidence to enable any prosecutions of the clearly guilty parties. If wishing a potential benefactor would die swiftly were judged a crime, half the country must be hanged tomorrow. Of crimes already committed, I can only say that having not been detected at the time, they are unlikely to be taken seriously now, in my experience.

There seems little point approaching those who wish to be widows and orphans. Their very lack of ready money has sent them on this path already, and it smacks a little too much of blackmail. Therefore, I must turn my attention to the eminent gentlemen who will undoubtedly wish to have the whole thing hushed up and disbanded without any public attention. I foresee that this year, a significant number of society figures will feel the urge to take the waters in foreign parts, until things quieten down. I suspect appointments to the farthest flung parts of the Empire are likely for certain young men. And for myself, a little more laboratory equipment and a few additions to my costume collection. On the whole, it has been a most satisfactory day.

§

Dear Professor,

When I grow up I want to be an experimenter, just like you, and kill people by blowing them up and making their heads fall off. If I am very good, Mummy and Daddy say they will let me have some puppies. What should I do first? From

Monty, aged eight and a half.

§

Mr Hoghmes,

As a man who works with the law, you should be aware that harassment is a criminal offence. We have the legal right to defend our property from unwelcome intrusion. The recent case of Crown v Trippet demonstrates that a man is well within his rights to shoot a boy who believes he intends to steal apples from his garden. Mister Spoon advises that you consider this carefully before loitering in our office doorway again.

Sincerely,
Alison Spoon

§

Professor Elemental. Mouse notes.

They do like cheese. A nice bit of Stilton goes down well. Very quick learners, when it comes to cheese. Not interested in little metal letters one bit.

Note to self: Get more cheese.

§

From the Diary of Algernon Spoon…

She came at dusk on the Friday, sweeping into my office like the gust of a tropical storm. She would have made other men sweat, and there was no doubt that when she went on her way, she might take anything with her. Women like Maude Plunkett hold a dangerous fascination. From the coquettish flash of booted ankles to the sultry gazes beneath lowered lashes, she knew how to work her wiles upon a man. But what she could not know was the manner of man she had tried to enchant. Algernon Spoon is not such a creature as to be taken in by a fair sorceress.

I played her game and let her think she was leading me, but all the while I was asking the questions, and her answers told me a good deal.

"Have you learned anything?" she enquired at once, leaning close to me.

"I have learned all manner of things this week, but the greater challenge lies in understanding which ones are of significance." There was a break at this point while she attempted to flatter me. I appeared flattered. We moved on. "Could you tell me something about the Goddingford fellow your brother alludes to? He sounds like a threat to your safety."

"Oh, Horatio exaggerates everything, poor dear. He and Goddy had a quarrel last summer, and he never quite got over it. I'm afraid he blames our old friend any time I am late returning home. You see, I like the city life, Mr Spoon. I am not cut out for a quiet, country existence. Horatio does not approve, and prefers to think all manner of silly things rather than admit that I am a rather modern sort of girl."

"I have no objection to modern girls," I said. It was evident she expected some ongoing flirtation on my part.

"I am very glad to hear it! I have no doubt you and I understand each other very well, Mr Spoon. Perhaps I should explain myself to you." She sat upon the edge of my desk. "I make my own way in the world. I like to think of myself as an entertainer."

I nodded. "I believe I understand you and shall, out of courtesy, be clear about my assumptions. You are a courtesan. I had suspected as much from the letters."

"Courtesan is a nice word, I think. It has a certain grace. I wouldn't argue with that assessment at all. You are a very smart fellow, aren't you?" she said, shifting her leg so that almost half an inch of stockinged calf was revealed to my gaze. "Goddy's an old chum. Quite harmless, I am certain."

I did not voice any alternative suggestions, although I must note here that the word 'strumpet' could have been created purely with this young woman in mind. "The neighbour who died was also a good chum of yours, I assume, since he left you so much money?"

"He was such an old darling," she said with a smile. "He was always giving me things. Even when I was a little girl, he liked to give me sweets and ponies and nice dresses. He was a dear." She sighed. "It's dreadful to think someone has killed him deliberately. He's an awful maniac, this professor. Quite mad. Have you got any evidence yet? Can we approach the police?"

I patted her leg. "It's not quite time for that; we need to have all our facts straight before it would be wise to make such a move. But you have been a great help to me already. There are a number of sinister influences in your brother's life that should be explored. The complexities of the Hermetic and Scientific gentlemen, for one."

"Oh, that's just a group of silly boys who like to get drunk together," she said with a most charming laugh.

"You are not aware, then, of the recent murders? The letters to your brother alluded to them."

She blanched and pulled away from me. "I thought that was said just to frighten him. I thought there was no truth in it."

"You come to town and yet you have not heard?"

Another pretty laugh. "Oh, I seldom take much interest in that sort of news. I rather prefer fashion and other people's scandals."

"The murders of other people can all too often be tedious," I observed, to her agreement. "Your friend, the old gentleman, did not consider himself in danger?" I added.

"If he did, then he never mentioned it to me, but he wasn't the sort of chap to tell a girl he feared anything. He'd been to India, you know. And he'd shot a tiger. With his bare hands."

Maude Plunkett

DISCREET HOSTESS SERVICES

"A formidable fellow, by the sounds of it."

There were a few more pleasantries before she departed. Was she in fact hiring me to frame this Professor Elemental, so that she could reap the rewards of her own murderous crime? Even when she laughed, the light never quite reached her eyes. I asses her to be a cold and calculating sort of woman, well-used to wearing masks. I understood her very well indeed. Could she be protecting an evil brother? Might she be in league with Elemental somehow? It wouldn't be the first time someone had hired my services with the intentions of scapegoating another. There will be no such goats courtesy of my investigations!

What troubles me most is that I cannot quite shake the impression that Miss Plunkett is telling me the truth, as best she is able. Her story is so unlikely, her manners so contrived to persuade, and yet I find myself a little persuaded. It is not in my nature to be overly moved by a pretty face or a neat ankle. I must further my researches into the Professor.

§

Mr Elemental,

We are writing to inform you that the badgermingos were entirely unsatisfactory. They ruined our game of croquet by eating the hedgehogs. We shall not be using them again and have returned to our own usual and dependable flamingos.

The badgermingos have all been beheaded and the same fate awaits you, should you venture into our domain again.

The Queen of Hearts

§

Dear Madam,

It is rare that I can become so angered reading a letter, particularly from a lady and a supposed royal at that. However, to have beheaded those sweet, reliable creatures, the badgermingos, is unpardonable. Each one of those beasts was created by my own loving hand, by slicing the head off a badger and... umm... oh. Yes, that's not much better, is it?

Ah well, we shall agree to call it even; I shan't pursue you through the courts for cruelty to augmented animals, and you must allow me to keep my head.

My dear brother can simply come to mine for tea and poetry for our next engagement. I have no desire to put one foot into your whimsical wonderland again.

Yours, etc. etc. and so forth,
Professor Elemental

§

Mister Hoghmes,

The written request that you desist in all attempts to speak with Mister Spoon was not an invitation to instead barrage me with unwanted letters. Please understand, I am not sympathetic to your case. I do not think that a collaboration with you is in Mister Spoon's best interests. I have no intention of assisting you in any way. Please go away.

Alison Spoon

§

From the Diary of Algernon Spoon...

That awful chap in the mouldering hat came round again today. I know he claims to be a private investigator, but as he spends the majority of his time hanging around outside my door, I think the title is more aspirational than actual. He has had one case that attracted attention, but it's all high society foolery and not anything of substance. I fear the only way I shall get rid of him is by finding him gainful employment. It's a sorry business.

§

Research Notes

Fatalities in Professor Elemental's Ipswich balloon crash – six in the balloon, two on the ground, one heart attack as a consequence of viewing the hideous events. Somehow, the Professor survived unscathed. Is he entirely human?

Deaths in stampedes caused by giant robots, vocal amplification, alarming lighting effects and other diverse sources of public alarm – seventy-three, including those who later died of their injuries.

Fatalities due to the private use of a Professor Elemental invention – nineteen that have been reported in the papers. There may well be others where the connection has not been recognised.

Non-fatal injuries due to the use of an invention: four-hundred-and-thirty-six, and no doubt going up all the while.

Fatal injuries at public demonstrations – five.

Fatal injuries at private parties – eleven.

Individuals burned or hung for witchcraft by their own community as a direct consequence of using something they had purchased from Professor Elemental – one.

Removals to asylums as a direct consequence of contact with Professor Elemental – three.

Parish priests known to have been required to perform exorcisms in response to something undertaken by Professor Elemental – forty-two, three of whom were in Spain. No records for other countries available in a language I can read.

There have apparently been at least seventeen direct requests for intervention to the Pope, but as the Professor is not a Catholic, admonitions from that quarter have had little effect.

Countries Professor Elemental is no longer legally permitted to visit – nine.

Foreign powers offering financial rewards for the head of Professor Elemental – two.

Death by Badgermingo – one.

Death by other creature purported to be in the power, scientific or sorcerous, of Professor Elemental – fifteen.

Evidence invariably anecdotal at best. Bodies are not always recovered. In parts of the country where Professor Elemental is known to have been active for months at a time, all kinds of natural disasters are attributed to him, including a plague of giant wasps, a man eating horse (could not ascertain whether that was a man who ate a horse or a horse that ate a man, though), numerous floods, one drought, one mining disaster, two factory explosions, seven mass poisonings, an outbreak of cholera and a missing sheep. It would seem unfair to entirely burden the gentlemen with responsibility for these incidents. But one never knows.

When one compares the figures with those of other eminent scientists, leading industrialists or especially persuasive electioneering strategies, the death rate for army recruits or some of the figures purported to represent deaths in foreign parts, the Professor seems quite modest in his aptitude for causing both death and mayhem. I am not wholly convinced that this assessment means he does not require further investigation. In question of culpability, I have no doubt that this individual has contributed to a good many deaths.

One does not prosecute the Queen for men who die in the army. One does not prosecute the police for those who mysteriously bleed to death whilst answering questions. One most certainly does not prosecute mill owners for dead children, mine owners for the occasional exploding of miners, or, God forbid, upstanding gentlemen like Indicative Johannes, who only last week set fire to three members of the public during a demonstration experiment into the use of some new chemical for ornamental purposes. It all comes down to intention. A man who does not intend to kill someone is not a murderer. He is merely unfortunate. It is interesting to observe just how unfortunate a man of extreme wealth can sometimes be in this regard.

§

Mister Hoghmes,

I appreciate that the business with the dog, and being so far from London, must be depressing for you, but really! Recall how keen you were to take this case. If you wish to be any sort of detective, it rather falls upon you to solve the mystery, does it not? You can't come running back to London for advice all the time. Mister Spoon is entirely occupied with his own clients and will not race off to the far ends of the country to help you out. He simply does not have the time. He suggests, however, that you take a good, hard look at the servants. Their grievances and motives are so often overlooked in cases such as these.

Sincerely,
Alison Spoon

§

Geoffrey,

Please pop into town and pick up the following at your earliest convenience:

6 x eggs

3 x tins of soup (bean and goat)

3 x tins of cellulose nitrate

Tomatoes

Basil

1 x crate of nitric oxide

Tetrafluorohydrazine

Tetrafluoroethylene

Tellurium hexafluoride

Toothpaste

Tuna (dolphin friendly)

Dolphin (tuna friendly)

Bananas (get at least 3 crates this time, and I WILL be

counting them)
   Wood (lots)
   Metal (some)
   Eels (around three should be fine)
   Large horse brush
   Large horse scissors
   Large horse
   All the cheese that you can find. Any type.

(...And don't use this list for 'intimate wiping'. I know you can read perfectly well. Or is it the badgermingos that left my 'Augmenting Apes: An Instruction Guide' book with the spine bent backwards and the page corners turned over on the chapter about the female ape form? No, it isn't.)

Yours etc. etc.

§

From the Diary of Algernon Spoon...

My charming landlady mentions that, as The Season is now upon us, she might easily find a more affluent gentleman lodger who keeps more reasonable hours and who does not so frequently soil the sheets with the bloody consequences of piles. I blithely pointed out that the finer the gentleman, the more unreasonable his hours must be, especially in The Season when so much entertainment can be enjoyed. I have little taste for it myself, but that is beside the point. To further amuse myself, I suggested to the vulgar woman – Mrs Lupinia Truculence – that piles are in fact all the rage this season since a certain royal gentleman admitted to suffering them, and one must always emulate the royals if one is to make a good social impression. Why else does she think so few ladies are wearing white? Dark skirts suggest that one may generate embarrassing stains, and so, like the black pox blemish of the beauty mark, they become fashionable.

Mrs Truculence is never entirely certain as to my seriousness. I recommended that she would need more fashionable curtains at the very least, if she meant to trade me in for a better quality of gentleman. New carpets would not go amiss, and her wooden furniture is easily a decade out of vogue. I think the woman is quite convinced that replacing me would be far too costly and time-consuming a venture to be worth the effort. Grand gentlemen all too often have grand debts, where I can be depended upon to pay my rent in a timely fashion. Hopefully, in all of this, the embarrassment of sheets will be forgotten.

§

Dear Mr Spoon,

Thank you for your recent enquiry; it is nice to have the opportunity to share some of the 'queer goings on' that have occurred, particularly around the proposed launch of my specially-commissioned water-slide.

As soon as I arrived at Mr Plunkett's, I knew that something was slightly amiss. My automotive 'legless horse' had no sooner arrived at the gates of his address when I was approached by a surly gentleman with virtually no neck to speak of. He gave me his name as Mr Murkin and told me that he was Mr Plunkett's manservant. (Manservant indeed! I have seen gorillas with a more refined appearance. One of Geoffrey's uncles has a particularly fine evening coat which put Mr Murkin's tatty butlering uniform to shame.) Murkin apologised in a thick cockney accent that we were "not allowed to use the main driveway as there 'as been problems wiv holes." He did not further elaborate what these problems were or the size of the holes. Still, I took him at his word and happily followed him into the surrounding undergrowth, eager to see my invention and meet Mr Plunkett.

After ten minutes or so of walking, I began to feel that we were getting further away from the manor house, rather than closer. It is well known that my sense of direction is second to none, particularly when travelling to the left – and I could feel something was up.

"Are you quite sure this is the right way, Murkin?" I

queried, as branches snapped into my face, taut from Murkin's ungainly passage through the woods.

"Hnnn," said Murkin in response, which I felt was rather unhelpful.

I raised my voice and caught up with his sizable frame, "Now listen here, man, I wish to speak to your employer, at once, or there shall be the most terrible trouble you can imagine. You should know that under my current trousers are some very different trousers created for a very specific purpose, and you won't want to see those. No, you will not.'

This seemed to grab his attention. He stopped dead in a clearing, silent except for the occasional chirrup of birds and the faint howl of a stoat in the distance. I stumbled into him and then gathered myself.

"Well, haven't you anything to say?"

Murkin stared blankly into the distance for a moment, then without warning, snapped back into the real world like a startled, but massive, hen.

"Of course, sir, sorry, I shall fetch 'is lordship right away. All will be explained, sir."

"That's more like it! And fetch me a drink while you're at it, there's a good chap." I had regained my composure and had a thirst for gin. Gin and answers. But particularly gin.

Murkin crashed off into the undergrowth and, after a moment or two, returned with a dirty glass filled with a queer-smelling liquid.

"There you go, sir." He grimaced while passing me the

glass; his smile looked like a dirty stretch of beach on a rainy day. "Is lordship will be wiv us shortly."

I eyed him suspiciously; there was something not quite right about this fellow, but what? I drank while I thought. Moments later, the trees seemed to take on a rich purple hue, as did everything else. I saw shadowy figures moving amongst the bushes, some with the heads of over-sized stoats, or so it seemed. I am not entirely sure *what* I saw, as I was gripped by a powerful fever. My mind blackened, I was adrift on a purple sea.

The next thing I knew, I was awake in my own bed. Plunkett hasn't replied to my most recent letters, and the address that I went to won't answer my calls, yells or screams. Nor can I find my way over the high fence that surrounds the property despite a number of painful, yet possibly quite comic attempts. I would contact the police, but after that terrible incident with the swans last year, I tend to steer clear of the gentlemen in blue. Besides, they would most likely attribute it to an over-indulgence of absinthe and, to be fair, nine times out of ten they would be correct. But not this time. I know my own mind – of that I think I am probably certain.

Most importantly, what of my water-slide? I worked long and hard on that, and a fine slide it is too. Apart from anything else, I would quite like a go on it.

Please do share any answers when they become available. I would like to know that my dear friend Horatio is alright.

He seems like such a nice fellow, and I want to make sure that no one has taken advantage of his kindly nature and relieved him of his fortune.

Yours etc. etc. sincerely and so forth,
Professor Elemental

§

From the Diary of Algernon Spoon...

Murkin? Surely it couldn't be the infamous Eddie 'Asparagus' Murkin, not seen for a good three years since he absconded with the Baron of Barnstable's jewels, the Baron's wife, and the Baron's mistress? Bodies were never found, but rumours abounded. It was assumed at the time that mistress and wife both were very likely sold into slavery in some foreign place where delicate English flesh is highly prized. Murkin was reputed to be a stocky man of common origins. What on earth would such a man be doing acting as butler in a country house? It seems most unlikely.

Or does our Professor suspect that I am on to him? Is this merely a ruse to distract me from the true crime? Oh, would that it were so! It would take a formidable mind to allude so casually to an almost forgotten fiend, testing my memory and merit, luring me with tainted bait. Let it be so! Or might it be that Murkin has hidden himself at the Plunkett abode? I shall make enquiries of Maude, and see what light may be shed. It was an oversight on my part not to consider the possibility of servants before. Murkin, positioned as a butler, would be well-placed to abuse the Plunkett family and take advantage of their financial gain. I see the makings of another complex plot. And another fine thought occurs. The Professor has not met Mr Plunkett in person; only Maude can vouch for the man's existence. What if there is no Horatio Plunkett? What if Murkin is behind it all? But why reveal himself to me in this way? Of course, no genius likes to go unnoticed, and that is so often where the criminally-minded fail. In hankering after recognition, they draw attention to themselves and pave their own path to the hangman's noose.

Surely I am not the only brilliant mind that does not crave public attention? I must ascertain if this truly is The Murkin. I must question Maude more thoroughly on the subject of servants. I must procure a new hat; this one is not presentable. I must write this list on another piece of paper to avoid confusion. I think my opportunity for using the Professor as a source of information has passed. But he is the centre of the case, the essence of the mystery. Unlock the mind of the Professor and, I have no doubt, all else will become plain. I must reflect on this; I do not see clearly how to proceed. Perhaps I must visit the Plunkett address myself.

§

Mister Hoghmes,

I am sending back the used deerstalker with no small feeling of revulsion. Never, ever, do anything like that again.

Alison Spoon

§

Dear Mr Elemental,

We have burned the designs you sent us, because, despite what we said in the advert, they turned out to be a bit too disturbing for our tastes.

Molly Libris
Secretary of The Women's League for Reformed Satanism

§

Dear Miss Libris,

I find I have lost track of our exchange. Did I send you designs for anything even slightly Satanic? I enquire because the Anglican Reformers League did not, it turns out, get my detailed suggestions for farming Irish orphans as a food source, and from the tone of their retorts, I fear I may have misdelivered the schemes intended for your good selves. Sorry! Can we start again, do you think?

Sincerely yours,
Professor Elemental

§

From the Diary of Algernon Spoon

There has been another Hermetic and Scientific murder. Of course, those in power are doing all they can to suppress news of it, for fear of what the poor, deluded public might do if they knew. Unfortunately, it is rather hard to hide something already witnessed by dozens, if not hundreds, of people in Leicester Square this morning. While the evening newspapers have been silent upon the subject, the public houses ring with talk of little else. A man found dead, impaled upon the horns of a living goat. And of course a scattering of clues to tell us that, if it is not the work of magicians, it is the work of people who would like to be considered magicians.

As yet there are no signs of panic-stricken riots or a mass exodus of the workers. One or two known Hermetic and Scientific gentlemen have taken the opportunity to retreat to their country abodes. Of course none of it looks good for them, and there are some who would see the wizarding orders closed down entirely. Based on observations to date, most of these are nothing more than clubs for chaps who like to roll up one trouser leg, put on a funny hat and have a secret password. It is the stuff of public school playgrounds and cheerful nurseries, continued into indolent adulthood, but it keeps so many of them out of mischief. Let them play at magic, I say! Otherwise, they may strike out into politics, and that would be in no one's interest.

Of course, no one hates the social wizarding set more than the true magi. I wonder if the violence comes from them? My contacts in that most secretive of underground networks are few, but informative.

Today I visited John the Retriever, the floating sage of Covent Garden. It's not easy talking to a fellow who insists on floating about at head height, but the sage is undoubtedly of the truly magical fraternity. He shuns publicity, but gives occasional and private demonstrations to the enlightened. I have had the pleasure of attending two such gatherings in the past and was impressed by his capacity to levitate through hoops – a feat that defies any mechanical explanations. He was of great help to me last year with The Business of the Missing Chickens in which we did detect an occult aspect. While that one was never properly solved, the problem did cease in a way that inclined me to feel it was a largely successful attempt on my part. Still, I would love to know what they did with all the feathers.

"What's the word on the ether?" I asked my magical source.

Wanted for Questioning

THE PUBLIC ARE ADVISED NOT TO APPROACH THIS SUSPECT

He produced a long, low and musical note, as is often his habit when composing his thoughts. "There is disquiet," he said.

"I am not surprised."

"Things which are not truly as they pretend to appear must always of necessity offence cause in the face of that which is fashioned innately from the fabric of truth," he added.

I wrote this down so as to be better able to consider it later.

"Not ready for the true powers, they jump at shadows and then are overwhelmed by horror when the shadows have no choice but to jump back, for, as it is above, so it must be below, and as it is to the left, so must it be to the right. All things in balance. All forms seeking truth. Do you understand me, young Spoon?"

"I am taking notes so that I can ponder your words at length."

"In knowing the limits of your ignorance, you have the makings of that which might yet be wise."

I thanked him.

"True wisdom knows here it shouldn't go meddling," he added. "The business of sages and mages is complex and not for you, my innocent friend."

On reflection, I feel that the floating sage has alluded to there being ill-feeling amongst his fellows in reaction to the faux-magician societies. Not that he ever says anything outright. I do not personally believe that the levitating in any way improves his powers of concentration. It looks very fine, but he has so few practical applications for it. He tells me that I have the mental discipline and psychic strength to become a sorcerer myself. Of course, it is pleasing to be told such things, but I cannot quite imagine I shall resort to conjuring just yet. Although, where the dead are concerned, it would provide a neat solution to the majority of murder cases. If necromancy replaces detecting, I shall of course shift my allegiance at once.

I see so many threads of connection here, but they are tangled, and may be no more than illusion. I have not been invited to comment upon the Hermetic murders yet, but as the police fail to make any progress, and the death toll slowly rises, I think it may be just a matter of time.

§

Professor Elemental. Mouse notes.

They are now all squeaking in tune with each other. That was a long, arduous day's work, but strangely satisfying. The chorus of their squeaks is lovely. Perhaps we should work on a Bach choral piece next? I see a future in choral mice, idea for small parties. Note to self: buy new trousers.

BWmfd94 miiiiiii vepslkdn3 gnld kwer ggg 76767676767

Note to self: Mice much more enthusiastic after being fed large quantities of sugary tea. Spellings leave something to be desired.

Note to self: I had assumed that the mice would understand good Queen's English as well as the next chap. Never had this trouble with the badgermingo. Had other, less trouser-friendly troubles, though. Mice easier on trousers. Smaller holes. No English. Must teach the mice to speak English! Wondering about other useful skills. Crochet? Tatting? I am pretty concerned about the ways of the mice, now that I'm getting to know them; their manners are appalling.

§

Dearest Professor,

Last night I stood under your window when it was dark, and I pulled my skirt right up so that anyone who was looking would have seen my ankles. You have ruined me forever. I know that you are a gentleman and will marry me at once.

Winny

§

Mister Hoghmes,

Your handwriting is unmistakable, even when you are incoherent. I return your most recent letter to me in the hope that, once properly sober, you will feel an appropriate degree of shame on reviewing your own outpourings. Please spare me the fruits of your ravings in the future. I will not be won to sympathy by them.

With regard to your recent exchange with my brother, Algernon says he does not have time to answer your correspondence himself and wishes you good luck.

I, on the other hand, wish you to sober up.

Sincerely,
Alison Spoon

Editor's note: the correspondence between Algernon Spoon and the lesser detective Steve Hoghmes has not come to light. Anecdotal evidence suggests that both Spoons destroyed all correspondence out of irritation, while Hoghmes destroyed his portion to avoid further humiliation. Only his unrequited infatuation with Alison Spoon allowed these letters to survive, allowing us a tantalising glimpse of the relationships that defined Hoghmes's career.

§

From the Diary of Algernon Spoon…

Maude came to see me this morning, radiant as ever, and keen for news. I asked her casually about the most recent

Hermetic murder, to see if her response revealed anything.

She replied, "Oh, it has nothing to do with Horatio's club, I feel sure. I think we must look to the magical men of London for an explanation. I hear they are dangerous, lawless creatures. Really, something should be done about them."

"One of the many social challenges of our time," I replied. It is one of my favourite stock responses, dependable to encourage clients to think I am in agreement with them.

"I have made several interesting breakthroughs with regards to your case," I said, once it was evident she had no news for me. "I think there is every possibility that your home has been infiltrated."

She gasped, a little too theatrically, I thought. "One of the servants?" she asked.

"They have access to so many personal things. Who is better placed to murder to your benefit and then pilfer from you? A servant, perhaps, working of their own volition…"

"Or planted in our home by that dreadful Elemental fellow!"

"Always a possibility," I conceded. "To proceed, it is absolutely necessary that I spend some time in your family home. I think the best solution would be if you pretend to hire me as a servant. Your brother need not know. It will give me time to properly survey the staff and to ascertain whether one of them has betrayed you."

She shook her head. "It is a ghastly thought. One pays people to serve, not to murder one's nearest and dearest."

I thought it best not to mention that, in my considerable experience, it is very usual indeed to find that just such an arrangement has been struck. "You agree to the plan, then?"

"Oh, Mr Spoon, I do not see how it can be done. The business of hiring male servants is entirely my brother's. I cannot imagine he would take a chap on my recommendation."

"I did not imagine he would, Miss Plunkett. No, you must hire me as your own maid. I am a master of disguise."

She stared at me with a most amusing look of disbelief upon her face. "You would never pass as a woman! You have a moustache!"

"I assure you that I have indeed passed myself off as a woman before and will again. Put your faith in me, and I shall not fail you."

"A man, as my maid… that would be…" She met my gaze, and I smiled at her.

"You are too much a woman of the world to be offended by such a notion. We shall mange well enough with the technical aspects of my job, I feel certain."

"We can but try. Will it not be dangerous, if your suspicions about the servants are correct?"

"I will not allow any harm to befall you, and I promise that if there is a viper in the family bosom, you will sleep safer for having had them exposed."

She frowned.

"The viper exposed. Not the family bosom," I clarified. "We should leave tonight. Can you permit me a few hours to make the necessary arrangements?"

"Shall I meet you here?" she asked.

I agreed.

§

Dear Mice,

Kindly stop singing to me in the wee small hours. I appreciate your enthusiasm, but really, chaps, this is not working. I know you can't read this and will just chew it and piddle on it and go back to singing, but it makes me feel better. If you had a shred of decency, you'd at least let me finish writing this before commencing to gnaw. Manners, gentlemen! You may be short, furry and obsessed with cheese, but it's no excuse!

Professor Elemental

§

My Dearest, Darlingist Professor,

You didn't come to my party! I feel that you have forsaken me. It was a charming affair. We had reached 'r' day in my revolutionary diet, and so there was rhubarb, radish, ravioli, reindeer, and a great deal of relish (gentlemen's relish, no less!). It's strange: I have lost a great deal of weight. Old friends barely recognise me. And my whole sense of the world is changing. I realise I can see right inside people, just by looking! Some of them are really lizards. Had you noticed that at all? More apparent after a few brandies, I find.

Dear Maude has come back with a very tasty servant girl. I do hope she'll stay. I know it's not dignified to notice the servants, but this one is a fox. Really. Red fur and everything. Big brush of a tail. Makes me want to chase her across fields and tear her apart with dogs. I'm not prone to romantic thoughts like this. I have the sudden and alarming urge to say 'rarrrr' a lot whilst rolling my Rs. Does that happen to you?

How are you, dear sir? Have you tried laudanum at all? I'm sure I'm getting shorter as well as thinner, now that you mention it. I am wondering if I might be light enough to float away if I jump out of an upstairs window? What is your professional opinion on this matter?

Yours in a bucket,
Horatio Plunkett

§

Mister Hoghmes,

I write on behalf of my brother to congratulate you on

the successful resolution of your investigations. We saw the reports in today's newspapers. Algernon asks me to express his gratitude for not mentioning his involvement to the press. He does not object to advising you on an ad hoc basis but very much wishes to avoid the limelight.

Sincerely,
Alison Spoon

§

Case notes: Eddie 'Asparagus' Murkin

Most prominent case involving Murkin occurred three and a half years ago, when he allegedly absconded with the Baron of Barnstable's jewels, the Baron's wife and the Baron's mistress. Some talk at the time of an insurance scam. The Baron did very well out of it, financially-speaking, although a lot of jokes were made at his expense.

Murkin repeatedly referred to in newspaper speculation of the time, no conclusive outcome.

Previously arrested on no fewer than thirty-seven occasions for theft-related crimes, but never actually charged. The nickname 'Asparagus' has to do with a complex bribery system. Murkin's contacts in the Vale of Evesham supposedly shipping illicit loads of asparagus into the city and using some of said to grease the palms of law enforcement officers to turn a blind eye. Must assume asparagus was thoroughly cooked first or else would have no application as a lubricant! Alison says I should not repeat that one as apparently it isn't very funny.

Black market in high-quality vegetables still thriving, some gang warfare after Murkin's absence created a hole. No apparent trace of Murkin remains.

Conclusions: He must have gone somewhere, but in this case 'underground' could equally mean 'dead'. Murkin is not the most unusual surname in the known world; this could just be an interesting coincidence. In which case we still have the assertion that something peculiar occurred to the Professor whilst attempting to visit Plunkett, or else the entire story is a fabrication.

§

Professor Elemental. Note to self:

How good are cats when it comes to training mice?

Mouse notes: I can't find any mice this morning. Cat has thrown all the metal letters onto the floor. Must find magnet. Mice are not the future – they are greedy little bastards with very poor manners and dreadful incontinence problems. There must be a more technological solution, involving lots of bits of metal. I suppose I'm going to have to invent something. It's so bothersome. Why can't someone invent something for me, just by way of a bit of variety?

§

From the Diary of Algernon Spoon...

The Plunkett establishment matches what little description I could extract from Professor Elemental's observations. Dense shrubbery abounds, and it is easy to imagine where the assault may have taken place. But of Murkin, I have seen no sign. Certainly, none of the indoor staff bear that name or match the villain's description. Nor have I caught ear of any distinctive cockney accents.

I find myself in a most peculiar household, though. Maude goes riding whenever possible and meets with friends, which has given me plenty of time to poke my nose into every corner. Horatio Plunkett does indeed exist, despite my concerns on that score. He matches the image created by his letters – a portly man in his middle years with no discernible chin, colourful waistcoats, and missing buttons. However, it also appears that he is either quite out of his mind or perpetually drunk. That might explain a good deal, but it hardly suggests him as a likely criminal mastermind. Unless, of course, he is a particularly talented actor. One never knows!

Plunkett sings loudly in the early hours of the morning. Yesterday, he rode a hobby horse down the long gallery and shouted to me that he meant to catch hold of my tail. Sexual predations could make my situation awkward indeed, but the man is heavy on his feet, and now that I am alert, I have not struggled to hide from him. Like a child, he is easily misled; curtains and the undersides of tables have sheltered me on several occasions, now. The more I see, the less I can believe he is the author of recent murders. I am inclined to agree with Maude's assessment that our Mr Plunkett is nothing more than a well-meaning fool. Albeit a drunken and slightly lewd well-meaning fool who currently believes me to be some sort of game creature.

§

Dear Geoffrey,

Do not expect me for afternoon tea, but do not take this as an invitation to eat all the biscuits. You should be pleased to hear that I have built a device for recording words. It weighs at least twice what I do and it takes about fifteen minutes a word. For speed and portability it remains unrivalled. I doubt your limited mind can appreciate what an amazing breakthrough this is. Never mind. I still won't be requiring afternoon tea, or high tea, or any other kind of tea unless there's some kind of alcohol in it.

I took the splendid new invention down the drive for a trial run, crushed a puppy, which you need to clear up, lost the letter M, which you can go and look for, and experienced a small explosion of uncertain provenance. Very pleased. Off to celebrate. If you work out what exploded, you can tidy that up as well.

I shall see you anon, if not somewhat later.

Professor Elemental

P.S., I may, of course, come back sooner, to make sure you aren't using this opportunity to do unspeakable things.

§

Professor Elemental, Progress Report

I have written this on y new recoding of words device, having scraped rest of the puppy off the inside. Still cannot find the letter after L, even inside puppy. Took a brief seven hours to scribe this. Reached end of drive. Exhausted. Giving up. Need tea.

Note to self: Burn typing machine, stamp on whatever is left, bury it in a deep pit and never speak of it again. After the entire day spent typing, I have come to appreciate the sheer joy of a decent pen dipped in leftover lunch for the recording of insights. Back to sound recording, I think; I was making better progress there.

§

From the Diary of Algernon Spoon...

Plunkett aside, this household gives every impression of being a fairly normal crumbling pile. The servants only work when they are being watched and fiddle the books at every opportunity. A great deal of good wine is consumed below stairs. I have been careful to participate enough to seem friendly whilst remaining sober. Several potted plants have suffered as a consequence, but no-one seems to have noticed this, either. The two sisters, Catherine and Matilda, are both very shy and retiring. They seldom speak, and wear veils, even around the house. I can see why Plunkett is struggling to marry them off. They lack Maude's vivacity and grace – both are more in the brother's shape and clearly lacked for sufficient dancing and deportment lessons in youth. They play the piano, take long walks in the garden, and retire to their rooms with headaches. Thus far I have not been able to get anywhere near them, but I fancy a conversation would furnish me with something of interest.

§

Professor Elemental, Mouse Notes

We want more stilton.

Apparently the mice are not all dead, have kept their letters, and are now leaving me messages. Well, at least the English lessons paid off, and I note a pleasing improvement in their spelling. It all comes too late for my typing machine, though.

§

Dear Professor Elemental,

Even though you are a patriarchal oppressor, we would quite like to buy some of your badgermingos. We would like some really angry ones. Females, for preference. Could they be trained to bite politicians, do you think?

Lady Maria Buckingly-Squatt

§

Professor Elemental, Note to self

Buckingly-Squatt badgermingo order. Must find use for leftover badger bodies. Geoffrey still angry about having to sort out all the dead goats. Badger hams? Badger handbags? Could make a lovely sporran out of a dead badger, probably. Gourmet meals with accessories? Whole new business horizons unexpectedly open before me.

Further note to self: Badgers unspeakably difficult to peel. Forget career in fashionable badger-based clothing. Cancel posters. Might be easier just to reanimate them in some new and terrible form.

§

Professor Elemental, Mouse Notes

If you ever want to see your cat again, bring us a whole Edam by midnight, love, the mice.

Dear mice, the cat was nothing but trouble, I will not bow to your demands.
Dear Professor, we have your new trousers.
Dear mice, look at this lovely Edam I found, do enjoy!

§

Mister Hoghmes,

At approximately three o'clock this morning, someone attempted a serenade beneath my window, utilising what I assume to have been a violin. The whole performance was wildly out of tune and an offence to the ear. It disturbed several of my fellow lodgers, all of whom are adamant that they saw you in the moonlight. Your recent exposure in the press makes you readily identifiable.

I do not begin to imagine what prompted this excessive gesture and can only request that you add this to the growing list of actions that are best unrepeated.

Sincerely,
Alison Spoon

§

From the Diary of Algernon Spoon...

In the early hours of the morning, I was woken from my napping by a tapping at my window. Something rapping, gently tapping, upon my window pane. It took me a few moments to collect myself. I did not open the window; I have read my share of gothic novels. (One.) Instead, I took a candle with the intention of reassuring myself. There was a face at my window. A strange and dark face like no other I have ever seen. The eyes were sad and luminous, the features strangely exaggerated. Then all at once, it departed. Could it have been a dream? Might the house be haunted?

This morning, I investigated the gardens and found signs of disturbance. The window to Horatio Plunkett's room had been left open. Coincidence? I think not.

§

Professor Elemental, Mouse Notes

Dear Professor, why don't you get a very big box and make a hole at each end?

Dear Mice, why would I want to do that?

Dear Professor: To feed the paper in. We type. We eject the paper.

Dear Mice? Forgive me if I sound paranoid, but what is in it for you?

Dear Professor: Cheese. No cat. We need more brie.

Dear Mice, are you proposing that we mislead people by pretending that you are a printing machine?

Yes.

Dear Mice, you are quite impressive chaps, why hide it?

Dear Professor, we like to mislead people.

Dear Mice: Are you really going to do my typing?

Dear Professor: We want a nice bit of gorgonzola.

Dear mice: You aren't, are you? You were playing with me, teasing me with your cynical type.

Yep. Cheese, or the trousers get it.

Note to self. Make mechanical cat.

§

Darling Maude,

So sorry we couldn't join you for an afternoon jaunt to the tea rooms, but I am afraid it is that time of the month again, and we are both suffering very badly with women's things and have to lie down a great deal. We hope you had a super time, so kind of you to think of us, but we are so very delicate and our poor feminine nerves could not bear the strain at present. We are just not as bold and vivacious as you are. We hope you do not mind too much,

Your loving sisters,
Katherine and Matilda

§

Professor Elemental, Note to self

Taxidermist chap at lecture said something about using tannin to preserve animal carcasses. Hard to hear the details over the screaming as the badgermingo and I were carried out. Tea has tannin in it. Steep dead badgers in tea until a use for them can be found. Get bigger tea pot. Get more tea. Remember where I hid the badgers. Nail flamingo heads to sticks and see how much use they are for croquette.

§

Dear Horatio,

It is with great haste that I get this missive sent to you by first post this morning. I have instructed Geoffrey to deliver it by hand and make sure that it reaches you, no matter what.

(He has taken his mission very seriously and is dressed all in black, while practising 'combat moves' and 'forward rolls'. It is rather distracting, truth be told, and I don't have the heart to tell him that in delivering this at first light, the all-black pyjamas will not aid him one jot.)

As your friend, your colleague and your investment, I urge you to put down the laudanum and come to the city. Let Geoffrey aid you if needs be (and if you can tolerate being dragged through the trees for several miles). I am beginning to become concerned for your safety and your sanity.

I am no stranger to intoxication; it is well-known that I once drank an entire bath of gin and was found hoisting myself up the flag pole on Windsor palace, all the while shouting 'God save the Me and all who sail in me!' over and over while crying uncontrollably. Nor am I proud of the six months I spent in the absinthe cafes of France in the company of a small army of imaginary green fairies who I blamed for the many atrocities I committed that year, most of them poetic. Indeed, I have even taken a trip down 'laudanum lane' as you are, now, and yes, I, too, thought I saw the lizards inside the flesh of men. I won't tell you how I found out that this is untrue. To be honest, I found out in a manner which was as regrettable as it was bloody.

I urge you, sir, come at once. Pack nothing but essentials: a change of clothes, some tea and plenty of money for incidental costs.

As for Maude and your new maid. Something tells me, sir, that you should watch your step around any new servants at the moment – women are trouble and women servants can be more trouble than they are worth. What do you know about her? Does she really have a tail? Are you sure? Well, then you are most likely wrong.

Shape up, sir. We have much to discuss, and I need you to have your wits about you. I want to share my recent experiences with you, but feel that it might not be safe to do so by letter.

Sincerely, your friend,
Professor Elemental

P.S. Do bring the laudanum. Just in case you are tempted to try it again, I can keep it and put it in a safe place. Or just take it one night while you sleep, so as to save you from temptation.

P.P.S. Don't forget to bring the money.

P.P.P.S. Or the laudanum.

§

Dear Professor,

He's so soft, your butler. So soft that I want to use him as a pillow. But he must fly. I did not know apes had wings, but how else did he climb to my window? I don't have long hair to dangle out and attract a rescuer, and that might be a bit girly. I don't have anything to dangle out. I feel I am in terrible danger. I am writing this note for Geoffrey to bring back to you, while he tidies my desk. Such a helpful fellow. Can you teach me how to fly as well? I will pack. I shall leave at dawn, count on it! I will bring everything. Ever.

Must dash!
Horatio

P.S. I think Geoffrey may have taken some of the laudanum. At least, I can't find any and he seems to be carrying a lot of frogs. Maybe I have taken the laudanum. I do love life's little mysteries!

§

Professor Elemental, Note to self

Get parrots out of bathroom. Get mice out of floorboards. Get mechanical cat out of the inner workings of the Gentleman's Moustache Stretcher. Find some new application for tea. Find trousers. Tea trousers? Why are mice obsessed with my trousers? Buy rat poison to put in cheese.

§

From the Diary of Algernon Spoon…

The house was in a state of utter chaos this morning. I gather from the cook that Mister Plunkett normally takes a cup of tea in his bedroom at nine am, and that the sisters Katherine and Matilda alone descend to consume a regular breakfast. Maude has a tray in her room when she feels like it – a tray it has been my cheerful duty to fetch. Plunkett eats randomly and sporadically. Apparently he is still experimenting with fad diets, and this week has refused to eat anything that was not a fish. Apart from plum pudding, which he has declared to be an honorary fish. He released two into the garden fountain to make his point.

When the cup of tea was delivered to Mister Plunkett's room at nine, he was absent and his things in terrible disarray. Given his eccentric habits, this was not considered cause for concern, initially. What caused some consternation, however, was the discovery of an escape rope made out of sheets and other bed-related fabrics, dangling from his open window. The butler soon established that it could not have been used to climb down – his brief attempt at impressing me by climbing up resulted in a bruised posterior and considerable damage to an ornamental rosebush.

Clearly Mr Plunkett wishes us to think that he has run away. Why go to such effort to create the illusion of a wild escape when one is master of the house and can simply leave through the front door at any time? The coachman has not seen him, though, and none of the horses are absent. Either Mr Plunkett is now hiding in his own home, or he is running cross-country on foot. Katherine and Matilda were so upset that they have retired to their room with smelling salts and are not to be disturbed. Maude is anxious and fears foul play.

Could there be something afoot here? Does the corpse

of Mr Plunkett languish on the property? Was the ladder an elaborate ruse, and if so, what end does it serve? We must consider that a villain is inside the house. It suggests there was merit in my servant theory. But which one? They all seem fairly harmless and about as foolish as your typical provincial serving types. I have not seen any who seemed above middling intelligence, and all appear happy with their lot. Or at least, happy enough not to be murderous.

"There are servants scouring the grounds," Maude told me, wringing her slender hands with anxiety. "I wish we could do more."

"We can," I assured her. "You and I should conduct a room-to-room search."

"You think he is still in the house?"

"If anything has befallen him, it would be a most natural diversion. The hopeless escape rope directing attention outside while other things happen inside. Now, while the chaos of a search commences, a murderer could easily hide the body."

She gave a pained yelp. "Do not say that!"

"Forgive me. That was less than perfectly diplomatic of me. It is the enthusiasm of developing a new theory. I allowed myself to be carried away for a moment. Of course, it may be that your brother has become confused and is lost, in which case a search of the house may discover him well, if disorientated."

She stared at me in blank disbelief. "Lost? In his own home?"

"This is a large property. It is not unthinkable. I do not think he has been in his wits for some time now."

She sighed. "He's not mad. We have all been distressed. Poor Katherine and Matilda have been almost bedridden with grief, except for mealtimes, and I myself have been finding it quite difficult to go cavorting about in my usual way. We are a household in fear! You cannot blame him for being a little distracted."

"I do not blame him at all," I said in my most reassuring tone. "At least if we search, we shall know. I suggest we begin at the top, and work our way down."

The Plunkett attics were dusty and littered with the usual lumber, but there were no footprints or other signs of disturbance.

"We do rather let these go to waste," Maude confessed. "Not so much as a mad relative up here. My brother has never been one to follow fashions that closely, though."

I managed to refrain from suggesting that he could perform the role of lunatic in residence very well himself, without the expense of hiring in a personage. It's as foolish as last year's trend for screeching jungle birds in bathrooms, and equally unconducive to performing essential and natural acts. Not that I am aware of any natural acts that would normally be performed in an attic space; a person of wealth merely stores servants or lumber in them, while a person who lacks wealth inhabits them.

§

Dear Madam,

I'm very sorry about what happened to your son, but really, he has only himself to blame. If he hadn't broken into my pantry and stolen the cheese in the first place, he would not have died in such terrible agony. I had poisoned that cheese for entirely legitimate reasons.

Sincerely etc.
Professor Elemental

§

Professor Elemental, Mouse Notes

Dear Professor Elemental, we have watched your failed attempts to poison us with more amusement than irritation. However, in the spirit of fair play, from now on you are going to eat a bit of the cheese in front of us when you deliver our dues. To check for poison.

Your friends, the mice.

Mice, damn you all, may the fur drop off your bottoms and unmentionable things grow there instead.

Professor Elemental.

§

Dear Professor Elemental,

I find myself obliged to write to you, although we are not known to each other socially. I find it my moral obligation to appeal to you, as a gentleman, to give up a course of action that has caused so much harm to so many.

As you are probably aware, your most recent commercial balloon flight to Ipswich crashed into the river, killing all those onboard and thus sparing them from the torment of experiencing the town. While we are relieved that disaster was averted this time, please pay more attention to the wind direction or land these reckless fools in Colchester. The strain placed on my mental hospital from those recovering from the horrors of Ipswich is already considerable; we can't handle the additional numbers your balloon flights have been generating.

Thank you in advance for your consideration,
Doctor Hemmingway Sockcrumpet

§

Dear Doctor Sockcrumpet,

I believe the simplest solution to your troubles would be to destroy Ipswich once and for all, sparing humanity from the horror and your asylum from over-population for all time. I should be very happy to sell you a small army of skilled and highly-trained minions, able to deliver tiny explosives in the shape of adorable children's gifts. I have a surprising number of exploding toys left over from a recent venture, and the making of a most excellent midget army, which would be yours to command and direct for a very reasonable sum of money. Of course, the technology is in its early stages and may explode at any time, and the minion army requires stern leadership and a strong stomach, and a lot of peanuts, but I feel sure a man of your intellect will be equal to the challenge,

Sincerely yours,
Professor Elemental

§

Professor Elemental, Note to self

Give badgers new heads and turn them into a lethal midget army driven by mad cravings for peanuts.

§

Dear Professor Elemental,

I am intrigued by the exploding children's gifts. Please do send a shipment at once. I am sure they will provide great amusement for my poor, traumatised inmates. Tempted as I am by your admirable plan to rid the nation of Ipswich, I fear I lack the youth and vigour such a heroic project would call for, but if I find a suitable chap to lead the way, you will hear from me at once!

Your friend,
Doctor Sockcrumpet

§

Professor Elemental, Note to self

Old shoes do not make good minion head. Plates break too easily. Badgers getting squidgy from all the tea but now smell faintly of bergamot. Can only pray the association does not put me off Earl Grey for life. That would be a tragedy indeed.

§

Elemental Toys

MAKE YOUR CHRISTMAS GO WITH A BANG!

From the Diary of Algernon Spoon...

I made a number of most interesting discoveries as we searched the house. We used some of the servant's doors and passages, and I 'accidentally' let us into Matilda and Katherine's shared rooms. Matilda and Katherine were absent from their rooms but had left playing a wax cylinder recording of themselves singing at the piano.

"That's 'I Wish My True Love Would Give Me His Ring'," Maude observed carelessly. "They're always singing that."

"Curious that they should leave a recording of themselves playing in their room while they are absent," I remarked.

Maude frowned. "That is a bit rum," she conceded. "Truth be told, they've neither of them been quite right since that awful business three years ago when they were held up by a highwayman. They hardly ever go out now, poor things."

"Was that when they took to wearing veils?" I asked, continuing to search their rooms for further clues.

"You know, I think it must have been round then, yes. The shock of it affected them both dreadfully."

"And would that be around the same time that they took up shaving, do you suspect?" I held up the tell-tale brush and leather strop.

Maude gazed at me, dumbfounded for several seconds. "Their legs, I must assume. It is something women do to make themselves more attractive to men, but that would be beyond the sphere of your experience, I imagine."

I said nothing and waited for her to continue.

"Yet they have spurned all suggestion of marriage, suitors and even the gentlest social gatherings. Why would they need to shave their legs at all?"

"Perhaps they have secret and inappropriate lovers," I suggested.

I watched her consider this, not wanting to jump to conclusions, but wondering about the absent sisters. "Where do you think they might have gone?"

"I can't imagine," Maude said. "They never seemed the types to have affairs, but perhaps I underestimated them. It would explain a great deal about their behaviour."

"I think it would be fair to say that your sisters have secrets," I suggested, but did not press further with my suspicions. There was only so much shock a woman like Maude could be expected to handle in one day.

The rest of the search afforded us very little by way of new insights. We established that Horatio was not in the building, but beyond that, all remained mysterious.

§

Beloved,

There is a new mole growing on my thigh in the exact

shape of your nose. I believe it is a sign from God that our spirits have been joined for all eternity. You will never be without me.

Winny

§

Professor Elemental, Mouse Notes

Dear Professor Elemental, just to let you know we have read all of your experiment notes. We think you are quite wrong about the talking machine. It will not work, much less catch on. Your friends, the mice.

Dear Mice, I am not going to be misled by you again! I shall persist and triumph. Or is this a double bluff? I think you think it will work but want me to think that it won't! But if you knew it wouldn't work, would you want shame and public ignominy for me? Of course you would. So you would encourage me to believe that it did work, but are you devious enough to attempt that by saying the opposite? You are scoundrels to the last furry, verminous one of you. I suspect you of imbibing coffee!

§

From the Diary of Algernon Spoon...

Two days have passed with no sign of Horatio. Matilda and Katherine are back in their room, or at least, they were seen at breakfast today and once again there is singing. They do not have the sweetest voices, I must observe. Maude is restless and disparages my skills at every turn. I fear I shall lose this case if I do not make a breakthrough soon. It is exhilarating to find that I may at last have met my match, and yet I am sorely disappointed in myself. Even if Miss Plunkett dismisses me, I shall continue to explore the case. I must know what has transpired here.

Attempts at finding further information regarding Matilda, Katherine and the highwayman have come to nothing. Even Maude seems uncertain as to where exactly they were when the incident occurred. It appears that, before this event, the younger girls were social butterflies and wholly occupied with the business of finding good husbands. Of course, it is possible that the adventure cost them their maidenhoods, and thus, shamed forever, such that they no longer feel able to seek a spouse. It is a story that makes sense of all the available intelligence I have upon them, and, yet, it troubles me enormously. I have presented myself at their bedroom door for many spurious reasons. Either they do not answer, and I find the wax cylinder playing, or they appear before me, heavily veiled. I have suspicions, but no proof at all.

I shall make a thorough search of the grounds, and if that

does not enlighten me, I think it will be time to return to London.

§

Dear Algy,

I hope no one opens this, and I hope it finds you well. All quiet here at the office. Walter Fibbets dropped in to pay for your work on the exploding mollusc case, and that chap with the awful hat came in again wanting your advice. I enclose all of the post that I've not been able to deal with – mostly it's been bills and payments this week, but I think these may be of interest, and potentially relevant.

I await your further instructions,
Alison

§

She is a gem, my secretary. A woman of insight and discretion, and one of the few living souls I have ever placed real trust in. This is in no small part because she is also my sister. The post she had forwarded for my attention was most interesting.

Mister Spoon,

I am not a man to be trifled with, and it has come to my attention that a certain pudding-esque quality has entered into our relationship. I speak of cream, and also jelly, which you should know that I take extremely seriously. I do not believe you are a book publisher at all, and that you have my letters for some other purpose. As you haven't tried to blackmail me yet, I have no idea what that purpose is, but be assured that I will not rest until you are well and truly thwarted! Unless of course you do intend to pay me, in which case we can undoubtedly skim over the thwarting and come to some understanding. That would be very nice, in fact. I prefer used bank notes but am amenable to any currency you care to name and not in the least bit averse to gems, gold bullion or stolen artwork. Not that I have any stolen artwork in my possession, I want to make clear, that was just to illustrate how very co-operative I am on the subject of payment.

In the meantime, I recommend that you explain yourself. Who are you, sir? What do you want with my letters? How did you come in to the possession of them? My dear friend Horatio assures me that he has not given them to you. He also assures me that no other person than Queen Victoria herself descended in a carriage surrounded by singing policemen in order to rescue him from recent danger, so it may be that his judgement is a little impaired.

Sincerely, etc,
Professor Elemental

Finally, my nemesis reveals himself! The letter is a work of genius. If I took it to the police, they would dismiss it at a single read, and yet all the ingredients are there: He intimates that Horatio Plunkett is both in his power and unable to think for himself. He demands payment. It is the most skilful and inspired ransom note imaginable. I see it all now. The Professor hires Murkin, who infiltrates the household and facilitates the daring kidnap. Through Murkin, others have been murdered to assure the Plunkett fortune and now, in this final, outrageous act, he strikes, taking Plunkett in order to receive the wealth his own devious murders have procured.

My God! It is inspired.

And yet in my heart I fear this may prove to be a case of wishful thinking on my part. At the very beginning of my career, I was hired to track down a missing heiress whom, her family believed, had been kidnapped by a rival family as part of an ongoing feud. I followed a trail of abandoned slippers, broken coaches, terrified footmen, and I met the young man who wanted to marry her and a whole cast of frankly rather unattractive stepsisters. From the threads of this I constructed a plot of Byzantium proportions and was saved from total public humiliation by sheer, blind luck. The girl had run off with her godmother, and although I was able to give the family reassurances of her physical safety, the decadence of her choice made them disown her. Not that I think she minded much about the money. Still, I learned my lesson. My work brings me into contact with depressingly few evil genius types. London is woefully short of criminal masterminds. My desire to find someone equal to me does tend to result in my seeing incredible, convoluted plots where instead I should recognise simplicity.

However, it occurs to me that my Professor-as-kidnapper scenario is the least insane explanation I can come up with at this moment.

Turning the letter over, I noticed something else written on the other side, in an entirely different hand:

Why don't you answer me? I shall die of a broken heart, and then I'll come back and haunt you and drive you mad with regret so that you drink poison and join me in death. That's how much I love you. Give me a sign that you understand.

Winny

Curiouser and curiouser.

I sat Maude down later that day and gave her a nice cup of tea.

"You've had some news, haven't you?" she said, rubbing her fingers together nervously. Was I right to stop suspecting her, or could this be her plot? Looking at her, I had to wonder if I'd been taken in by her style.

"I've received a letter which suggests that Horatio is now in the company of Professor Elemental."

"Kidnap!" she whispered, her eyes growing round with alarm.

"That was my first thought, but perhaps we should not leap to conclusions."

"Do you have any other explanation?" she demanded.

"Not as yet, but I prefer to keep my options open. I propose that I go to the Professor's house and speak with him, man to man, as it were. I will seek some evidence that your brother is alive and well, clarify the terms of Elemental's demands, and see what can be done to resolve matters. In the meantime I suggest that you return to London or go to friends."

"You do not think I am safe in the house?"

"Frankly, I do not."

"But what of my sisters? We will never persuade them to leave."

I had spent hours trying to work out how to break this to her. "I do not think your sisters have lived under this roof for a good three years now."

"That's utter nonsense."

"Listen to me, Maude. The highway man, the veils, the shaving equipment, the sudden loss of interest in social gatherings."

"I don't understand."

This bit of the plot, at least, I felt certain of now. Admittedly most of the evidence was circumstantial, but it fitted together too well.

"Three years ago, something terrible did happen to Katherine and Matilda. They never returned to their house. Instead, a well-known criminal by the name of Eddie

'Asparagus' Murkin, and some equally dubious companion of his, returned in their place. When I first spoke of infiltration, I did not imagine the scale and audacity of the plot, but think of the wax cylinder, think of the evidence."

"My God," she said, and in the heat of her emotion, knocked over the teacup. Brown liquid spread over the immaculate tablecloth, and we both stared at the growing stain as though it were blood. "Then my sisters?"

"I do not know. Three years is a long time. They might have been killed; we would not find identifiable bodies. They could have been taken to any number of places. The fates of young women in such scenarios are likely to be unhappy."

"I had no idea. We were never close," she confessed. "Oh, but I have failed them." She wept bitterly, and I think her tears were real enough.

It turned out that my ice queen had a heart after all, and it ached for the fate of her unfortunate sisters. I did not mention the probability that they had been forced to work as prostitutes and had probably died of venereal diseases by this time. There are some things it is better not to know.

Maude clutched my arm, her eyes full of desperation. "Save my brother!" she begged.

"I will do everything in my power," I promised. "First, we must see you to safety. You had best pack."

§

Professor Elemental,

Please stop encouraging people to use our fine tea as embalming fluid. It's just not cricket, and the Worcestershire sauce fellow has threatened to sue for infringement of funereal comestible law.

Sincerely,
Fustram Mapplethwait

§

Dear Mr Mapplethwait,

I must apologise for the confusion, and blame the newspapers entirely. I have yet to test your excellent teas with regards to their long-term embalming potential. I can, however, entirely recommend them for badger preservation. I think you underestimate the potential sales for a product that can both keep a badger from decaying and stop it smelling quite so much like a badger. How many dead badgers are there in England, desperately in need of such treatment at this very moment? Think of it! Think of the sales! Think of sending me a cheque in thanks for my efforts on your behalf. Or more tea. I've got through a frighteningly large amount of tea with this badger business, and at least some of that was on your behalf, so I rather feel you are in my debt.

As for the Worcestershire sauce chaps, who do you think it was that first established the use of their product in the field of mortlessness, eh? Who else would have the audacity, nay, the genius to pump the body of a recently-deceased vicar full of that strange, fishy concoction? Me! I thought no one could possibly have forgotten my vital role in that historic discovery. If they give you any trouble at all, tell them they are welcome to commission me again. That should settle them down.

Sincerely etc,
Professor Elemental

§

Professor Elemental, Note to self

Tea… cricket. I can almost smell the connection. Cricket tea? Tea for crickets? Sometimes I feel so clever I almost wet myself.

§

From the Diary of Algernon Spoon...

As the train carried me from London to Professor Elemental's infamous country pile, I remembered the second letter Alison had forwarded. It read...

I would like to hire you to help me track down a missing dog. I am very fond of the dog, and the pay will be excellent. I require absolute discretion.

Archibald Mandrake
Grand High Vizier of the Guild of Modest Men.

This troubles me. I do not like it at all. No one pays my kind of rates to seek out a dog. I imagine it must be a convoluted way of expressing something else entirely. Usually such mysteries draw me in, but I have a gut feeling that this is a case better ignored. Perhaps I can direct them to my friend with the terrible hat. Word on the street is that he'll take anything, having a costly drug habit to sustain. A man of vices is all too easily manipulated. I shall decline this one. Anyway, with the Plunkett business still unresolved, I am in no position to hunt for errant dogs, be they ever so symbolic.

I was fortunate in finding a farmer willing to give me a ride on his cart from the train station towards my destination. Mercifully he was bearing only the scantiest remains of vegetables, and I was spared too much direct contact with the outpourings of nature.

"Going up the big house then, are you, sir?"

When I confirmed, he sucked on his teeth. "It's not my place to comment on my betters, mind you."

I nodded, "I quite understand. The Professor must be an influential man in these parts."

"Not so much that," the good yokel replied. "But they do say as how he gives folk the evil eye, and if you upset him, he sets his terrible giant hound on you. It's a great big hairy thing, like a man-dog. Might be it's a Frenchman. Wears a jacket, but I tell you something, be it man or beast, it's not from round here."

I wished him good day and made the final part of my journey on foot. How to proceed? Stealth and observation? Could I find and rescue Plunkett? Or should I meet the Professor face-to-face and see how he envisaged his convoluted scheme playing out?

There, on the lawns before the great house, I saw a naked man engaged in a profoundly unnatural act with the facsimile of a human figure. He spotted me at once. The hideous, flabby form wobbled towards me, and I covered my eyes in a futile attempt at self-defence.

"You look like a fox! Which is damnably funny because only last week I had a servant girl who looked like a fox too. Well, not so much "had", in the Biblical sense, although it wasn't for lack of trying." Horatio Plunkett slapped me on the shoulder.

"Good day to you, Mr Plunkett," I said, gathering what composure I could. "Are you well?"

"Never better. Just testing out this Teach Yourself the Exotic Dances of Far Flung Parts of the World automaton. Think she needs a better name, but she's got all the moves, eh?"

"That was dancing?" I enquired, trying to blot the awful remembrance from my mind.

"Exotic dancing," Plunkett reiterated. He seemed perfectly happy, and entirely out of his mind. "Come in, have a nice cup of tea," he added. "Geoffrey can brew us up a pot. Splendid fellow. Knows the Queen."

Conscious that both my mind and my body might be at risk, I followed him across the lawn and into the house, doing my best not to see the undulating expanse of his pastry-like buttocks.

§

Professor Elemental!

Oh God, sir! Now we hear that you advocate people use our tea to eradicate infestations of crickets. Are you doing this on purpose? Have I in some way offended you? Please, please stop talking about my tea – you are bankrupting me. I cannot sleep at night for fear of what you will say next.

In desperation,
Fustrum Mapplethwait

§

Mr Mapplethwaite,

Really, what possibly is there not to like about the power of your excellent tea, revealed in all its glory? Who cannot say they are driven mad by the infuriating sounds of cheerful little insects going innocently about their business? It is the very bane of a country summer, and I feel certain that Lords and Gentlemen across the land will delight in silencing the little horrors by my method. Our method. With your tea. Fired from my steam powered tea gun. I grant that reports of the scalding incident are a setback, but you must put more faith in the great British public and my new array of posters. Patience, good sir. Rome was not burned in a day. Although, now that I think about it, it probably was, and I have no doubt that, as they ran from their burning homes, the good people of Rome could still hear all those happy, chirpy crickets and would have sold their very souls for the means to destroy them.

I am sure you now understand me perfectly.

Professor Elemental

§

Teach Yourself the Exotic Dances of
Far Flung Parts of the World Automaton

From the Diary of Algernon Spoon...

There had been references in the letters to a monkey butler. I assumed it would turn out to be some kind of dreadful, racial slur. My experience of the upper classes is that they all tend to consider the less wealthy to be on the level of animals. Horses and dogs are better cared for than the human animals who are sent up chimneys and down mines. The monkey butler shocked me to silence, for I must observe that he was unequivocally not of the human race. Furthermore, as he presented us with a pot of tea and some very nice biscuits, there is ever a case to be made for his indeed qualifying as a manservant. It was most perplexing.

The house contained more unfamiliar items than even my sharp mind could catalogue. Some of them moved, with steam and clanking noises issuing from their curious forms. Others crawled and whimpered in a most unsettling manner. Evidence of a mad genius at work lay on every surface. Plunkett might have the madness angle covered, but from the way he was singing, I had every certainty he did not contribute genius to the arrangement. Observing him, it was evident that he felt at home, and there was nothing aside from perhaps the monkey butler and the nudity that prevented him from leaving.

"Are you happy here?" I asked Horatio.

He dunked a biscuit in his tea, put it back on the plate and ate one of the dry ones. "He's my true, good, dear, perfect friend."

Steam Powered Tea Gun

FOR THE MODERN GENTLEMAN

"Do you mean Professor Elemental?"

"I do! A giant amongst men. I have never been happier."

I considered the scene. It was possible that unnatural substances had poisoned his mind and created this unhinged state. Equally, he may have been barking all along. What little I saw of him in his own home suggested as much.

"Maude is concerned about you," I said gently.

"Maude is made of spoons," he replied.

"Shall I reassure her that you are well, and safe?"

He tipped the last of the cooling tea into his groin and smiled. "Please do. Dear little mouldy Maudy. I used to call her that when she was a girl, and she used to punch me in the testicles. Happy days!"

I wanted to ask him about Katherine and Matilda, but in his confused state, it did not seem wise. Having determined to take my leave and report back to Maude, I rose. It was then that I saw him. He was skipping down the hallway beyond the parlour in which I sat. I rose, transfixed by the unlikely figure. In my mind, the Professor had gained epic, near legendary proportions, in no way resembling the strange form approaching me. And yet I knew, none the less, that our paths had finally crossed as destiny had long demanded that they must. I stepped forward to meet him.

"Professor Elemental, I presume."

He eyed me cautiously before accepting my hand. "The very same."

"He's a fox," Horatio called out from behind me. "Found

him on the lawn, couldn't resist the bushy tail, knew you'd understand. There isn't any tea left."

"Well, if you will keep trying to bathe in it," the Professor replied, his tone betraying a hint of strain. Then he looked at me again, the expression calculating. "Who did you say you are?"

It might have been expedient to lie, but in that moment, I wanted him to know something a little bit like the truth. "Algernon Spoon."

"Ah ha! And you don't even look like a book publisher. I knew it!"

"What do I look like?" I enquired, wondering just how perceptive he was.

He leaned to one side, contemplating me. "Not a fox, either. I have to disagree with you there, old chum."

He smiled like a man who has just unravelled a most delicious secret and is not planning on sharing a word of it. I felt unnervingly exposed. "Well, sir? How do you asses me?"

"You clearly aren't here to collect a debt. You've been far too polite for that. Nor do you look like the type to try to buy something. What does that leave us? Are you a reporter, by any chance?"

"Close." For a heart-stopping moment, I wanted him to see right through me. To have someone recognise my secrets, and the genius of my game. This can be a lonely business.

I had walked in to the house expecting to negotiate over the kidnap of Horatio Plunkett, but the man looked entirely at home. I therefore had no idea what I was doing. It was a strangely liberating state to be in.

"You owe me a letter," Professor Elemental remarked, turning to kick something that had emerged from beneath the nearby cupboard. "Or at least an explanation."

"I lied about the book," I said.

"A shame. That would have been entertaining. So why are you collecting my post? There's no point trying to blackmail me: I don't have any money, and I don't need any help ruining my reputation, thank you very much."

"You have that entirely in hand?" I ventured.

"Precisely."

I liked him, God help me. I do my best to avoid liking people. In my line of work, it only leads to trouble. The evil genius, the kidnapper, maker of plots, killer of maiden aunts... I could not quite reconcile the fellow before me to any of the images I had built of him over the months. What on earth did that leave me by way of options? I resorted yet again to telling the truth, conscious that I was courting a habit I could ill-afford.

"I'm a private investigator. It appears that someone may have been attempting to frame you for murder."

"That's rather an unsporting thing to do," he said. "Is this someone I've offended? It wasn't because of that business with the inflatable lion pen, was it?"

I had no idea what he meant.

"Am I going to need to change my trousers?" he enquired.

"Not imminently, but it might be as well to apply some to Mr Plunkett."

I stayed for nearly an hour and then telegrammed Maude to assure her that Horatio was safe. I did not reveal his location.

§

Last night I dreamed I was sniffing your pith helmet.

Winny

§

My dear Fustrum,

Have you read the newspapers today? The recent, albeit failed, attempt to rob the Swyving Bank in Peckham last night featured not only my steam-powered guns, but also your most excellent tea. Did I not promise you fame and success? Now that the criminal underworld has become alert to your tea, you will no doubt be in great demand, a veritable celebrity. I had a nice chat with the police this morning and assured them that I'd never met a criminal in my life, at least, not in a professional capacity, and that either I had sold the guns in all innocence, or they had been stolen from someone else. Apparently they are effective against people as well as crickets!

Do you have any connections in the Admiralty? My previous army contact recently eloped with his horse, but there must be military applications for scalding hot tea, your own, most excellent tea, fired from one of my devices.

The world shall not forget either of us, Mr Mapplethwait!

Your good friend,
Professor Elemental

§

Dear Professor,

We are impressed by the quality of your work and hereby invite you to join the Secret Alliance of Hermetic and Scientific Gentlemen. Membership is free, but you need to bring your own apron and decide in advance which part of your anatomy is to be branded with the sign of our elite brotherhood. We look forward to initiating you.

Your friends,
The Secret Alliance of
Hermetic and Scientific Gentlemen

§

Dear Hermetic and Scientific Gentlemen,

I should like to make it clear that I was flattered and delighted by your letter and that I think very well of you indeed, and your goats, and that I really, really do not want to die in some dark place and by profoundly unnatural means. Come to that, I'm really not keen to explore dying in any context at this time. I do read the papers, you see, and I have heard as much about you as you clearly have about my own highly acclaimed and excellent work. I don't wish to imply that you are those sorts of Hermetic and Scientific Gentlemen; you may after all be very nice fellows with no interest in either goats or hideous ritual murder. But if you were, I should like you to know that I don't have anything against you at all and am very keen not to cease breathing. As I cannot tell whether it would be safest to decline or accept your lovely offer, can I say 'maybe' and have a little time to think about it? Say, thirty years, for due and detailed consideration?

Sincerely,
Professor Elemental

§

Plunkett Case Assessment

Horatio Plunkett is not in his right mind. Was this always the case? Has he been poisoned? Is someone else manipulating him? If so, who? Maude stands to benefit the most. I must not rule out Elemental.

I am absolutely convinced that the sisters Katherine and Matilda were kidnapped three years ago and replaced by Murkin and his sidekick. All of my evidence is circumstantial. A medical examination would only prove gender, not identity. Who is to say they were not men all along? Without evidence, there is nothing whatsoever I can do. They have the house; what is to become of my clients? How much will I be expected to resolve?

Is someone trying to frame Elemental for murder, or is it simply that his devices are a convenient way of disguising the intent to kill? With so many people mad for science, and so many deaths and injuries, it's an easy way to hide a psychotic agenda. Is the Professor himself to blame, a combination of bluff and truth bound together such that he seems like a harmless, inadvertent killer of hundreds when in fact he has been doing it deliberately all along? Where does the monkey butler fit into this? What unnatural or uncanny procedure enables a mere ape to make the perfect cup of tea? There are so many people with reason to hold a grudge against Elemental – the maimed, the bereaved, the Mapplethwait Tea Company, the now defunct Haversham Zoological Gardens, where three people died after the recent failure of the inflatable lion pen. Everyone in Norwich. Rather a lot of people in Ipswich. If the motive is to destroy this man, the potential suspect list is extensive, to say the least.

Goddingford. A name and nothing more. A loose end I should perhaps look at more carefully.

The Hermetic and Scientific Gentlemen, Venerable and otherwise. The murders. I can't assume this is wholly unrelated, because Horatio holds membership. Could, of course, be a coincidence. It may be one of those games that went too far, drunken dares and high jinks. It is also very high profile, and solving it would risk attracting attention, and that does not sit well with my business plan, however much it may appeal to my vanity.

Winny. That scrawled note on the back of a letter. Or did the Professor write on the back of her letter to him? The latter would suggest total disinterest; the former implies that she has access to his house. She will die of a broken heart? And that first piece, tucked in with the initial Plunkett correspondence. A forward approach that suggests a lack of concern with social convention at the very least. Winny, who loves him so much, she wishes him dead. The human heart motivates so many crimes and makes very little sense to me. Winny bothers me, and I do not quite know why.

The whole thing is a bloody convoluted mess. I cannot quite believe that anyone would have planned the entirety of it.

§

Mister Hoghmes,

In answer to your question, no, Mister Spoon tells me he is not directly engaged with the mystery of the Hermetic and Scientific murders, but he is following them with interest. He promises that if any theories occur to him, he will not hesitate to inform you.

Sincerely,
Alison Spoon

§

Dear Professor,

I accidentally purchased your self-loading sausage machine, wrongly believing it to be a work of modern art and not a technical device at all. It loaded my employer. I cannot think you enough for the joy and peace your inspired invention has given me. Forgive me for withholding my name, but I do not wish to attract direct attention.

Editor's note: Nothing has been discovered corroborating this claim. However, the proper authorities have been informed. They had a good chuckle and suggested this would count as death by misadventure and not murder, and that I should not have interrupted their game of backgammon with something so trivial.

§

Dear Professor Elemental,

We can only advise you that it would be entirely in your interests to align yourself with us. The Anglican Reformers League has put a price on your head after you caused them to partially build a Satanic temple rather than the ethical orphan-farm of their dreams. It takes a man of no small genius to lure these gentlemen into an act of accidental Satanic homage and we do, quite seriously, salute your genius and wish to protect you from danger at their hands. We would also like to buy some steam guns and were advised that you had sources for bulk-buying goats.

Sincerely,
The Scientific and Hermetic Gentlemen

§

Hunt For Missing Gentleman Continues

Is Horatio Plunkett the latest victim of Hermetic and Scientific crime? Reported missing last week, Plunkett's disappearance has caused widespread consternation. Does he join the ranks of murdered club members? Will we soon discover his body, arranged in some truly macabre way? We think of poor Henry Lewis Smuttingpaddle, dead on the horns of a living goat. Rumour has it that Plunkett may have been kidnapped, but no demands have been released. Certain gentlemen, who wish to remain anonymous, have suggested to your reporter that Plunkett himself is entirely to blame for the recent spate of Hermetic crimes and has in fact fled the country to evade detection and punishment. With some of our most eminent crime solvers taking up the challenge of this case, it can only be a matter of time before the truth is revealed.

Plunkett himself is a man of curious history, having inherited his fortune after the untimely deaths of a number of relatives. His sudden rise to affluence might cause a suspicious mind to wonder at the precise nature of those deaths, and the frequency with which tragedy has haunted his immediate family. A prudent man might not wish to make public having bequeathed any sum to Mister

Horatio Plunkett, we suggest.

In the meantime, the police advise all persons who are concerned for their safety to take the following precautions whilst in London: Avoid goats. Wear a sensible coat rather than anything that might be mistaken for robes. Avoid travelling alone after dark. Do not paint quasi-mystical symbols onto yourself, your property or your children. Do not accept offers to dinner from strange men wearing cloaks painted with mystical symbols. If you see anyone dressed as though they intend to participate in ritual murder or sacrifice, do not approach them directly, but, instead, make with all due haste for the nearest police station where you can have a nice cup of tea and leave it to the professionals to sort things out.

Furthermore, it will reassure you to learn that the fine gentlemen of the police have made a number of arrests in connection with this case. Detective Sergeant Augustus Mentionables revealed this morning that several individuals are now 'helping with questions' but declined to give any names. He reassured me that they are making excellent progress, and expect to have some kind of breakthrough for us very soon. Five goats have also been taken in for their own protection.

§

Dear Professor Elemental,

We, The Mostly Pacifist Anglican Reformer's League, wish to save your soul from Satan's dire grasp. Like many young men of our time, you may have succumbed to temptation, imagining the occult to be no more than superstition and an amusing game for rich young gentlemen to play at. You may think that black magic is nothing more than harmless entertainment. We find ourselves morally obliged to point out to you that, unlike high fashion, laudanum and social archaeology, Satanism imperils your very soul and will cost you your eternal life.

We can save you!

Membership of the League is free, but you need to bring your own apron and decide in advance which part of your anatomy is to be branded with the sign of our elite brotherhood.

Yours, in Jesus Christ and a really nice hat,
The Mostly Pacifist Anglican Reformers

§

Mister Hoghmes,

Augustus Mentionables

LEAST EFFECTIVE CRIME SOLVER OF THE YEAR

I must beg your forgiveness, having just received your letter. I had assumed that the gentleman's undergarments pushed through the office letterbox belonged to you. Given your track record, it was not an unreasonable conclusion to draw. I did not send them out of any desire to see you wearing them, and I suggest that you dispose of them as you see fit.

Sincerely,

Alison Spoon

§

Dear Professor Elemental,

I am writing to you on the instruction of my brother, Algernon Spoon, who I believe is known to you. Yesterday morning, my brother was arrested by the local constabulary. I was present at the time of the arrest, and he asked me to tidy up the case left open on his desk. I only had a few moments before the police started confiscating files, but the letter on his desk, on which he had been working that morning, was addressed to you, and so I imagine it is you that he wished me to contact. I was not able to salvage the letter, though, as the police have taken it.

It is my understanding that Algernon has been arrested in connection with the disappearance of Horatio Plunkett, and, from comments made by my brother, I think it is the case that Mister Plunkett's whereabouts are known to you. If Mister Plunkett would make contact with his sister, or the police, this would help us significantly.

I do not know in what capacity you were corresponding with Algernon, but you should be aware that your letters to him are now held by the police, and that they appear to be looking not only into Mister Plunkett's disappearance, but also into the Hermetic and Scientific murders. I am sorry to say that Algernon was arrested on suspicion of murder, kidnap and the abuse of goats in public places. He was composed as they led him away, his only words 'tidy up the case I had open on my desk'. If you are in any way a friend of my brother's, I must ask for your assistance. Due to his line of work, Algernon has not always been popular with the local constabulary, and I am concerned as to what scores may be settled while he is behind bars. Algernon is not as tough as he often seems, and I worry for him.

Sincerely yours,

Alison Spoon (secretary)

§

Dearest Alison,

You don't happen to be unwed, under fifty and open to romantic propositions, by any chance? I ask because you are my first female correspondent this week who does not appear to be a) totally mad b) trying to blame me for something I really didn't do c) trying to convert me either to or from Satanism.

Well, this is all very confusing, isn't it? I have indeed exchanged a few letters with a chap called Algernon Spoon; he said he was a book publisher, and then he said something else, and not so very long ago he turned up at my house, so he knows perfectly well that Horatio Plunkett is currently living in my larder and playing havoc with the dancing lady automata. We lack for female companionship here at present, which in Horatio's case is probably just as well, if his methods for courting robots are anything to go by. He may be a little confused, but he lacks gallantry. I, on the other hand, am well-versed in the skills of romance and rather in need of something other than badgers for solace. Not that I use the badgers for solace, I hasten to add. No, not at all. But they are very pretty. Do you like badgers?

But you didn't write to me to discuss the finer points of badger grooming, nor, I suspect, in the hopes of being wooed. Obviously, if you would like some Professorial wooing, I have an exciting new pair of trousers that I have yet to try on anyone. Do, do say if I could tempt you to a nice cup of tea and a trouser viewing.

I have asked Horatio about making his whereabouts known, and I'm afraid he responded by getting under the nearest table and putting a bucket over his head. It was unfortunately the bucket Geoffrey had been keeping his eels in, so we've had a rather busy sort of morning, punctuated by screaming and slithering, and I am answering my post in stages. Have I propositioned you yet? Ah yes, I have, moving on then… Horatio is safe. At least, as safe as a man can ever be with a laudanum habit and an eel down his trousers – and that's not a euphemism. I saw it peering out over the top of his shoe not five minutes ago.

Obviously I'd like to help your brother. I have absolutely no idea what's going on, however, but it may interest you to know that I've been building a midget army for some time and have been looking for the right buyer for them. Perhaps we could use them to break into the prison and free Algernon? I still have a few exploding toys lying around the place. I wouldn't be doing the exploding or jail breaking myself, of course, but can supply raw materials and some suggestion as to how some of it works.

In the meantime, are you busy at all next Tuesday?

Sincerely yours,
Professor Elemental

§

Mister Hoghmes,

I do not believe that the crime of the mystery undergarments is worthy of investigation. Let us try and forget the whole sorry business. I assume you have not read the papers and are unaware of our current difficulties?

Sincerely,
Alison Spoon

§

Dear Professor Elemental,

What a delightfully amusing situation we find ourselves in! We have in our possession a charming young lady by the name of Maude Plunkett, who firmly believes that you have kidnapped her brother. We have no idea what you have or have not done with good old Horatio; he's rather slipped through our fingers. While this is a source of some irritation to us, it does not constitute an insurmountable problem.

Here is what we propose: You keep Horatio, use him as you see fit. He's probably a bit doolally, and there's no knowing what may happen if he doesn't get his usual opium fixes. He is accustomed to receiving very small doses at regular intervals, but is not quite aware of his own medical needs. For our part, we will continue to take care of sweet, lovely Maude, who has turned out to be very accommodating with regards to our many and complex needs. Do, do intimate this to your guest; we would like him to have some sense of the degree to which we have debauched his entirely willing sister.

If Horatio tries to remove us from the house, we will make public the wax cylinder recordings that chart Maude's frankly animalistic behaviour. We should also make clear to you that Horatio Plunkett has no way of proving his identity or drawing on his own resources, and will be depending on Maude to publically identify him. Oops.

You have no need to trouble us; kindly stay away from the property, and we will give you no further difficulty,

Now, how to sign off?

Think of us, please, as Katherine and Matilda Plunkett. And think, also, that Katherine and Matilda are very good names for large, hairy men with a good working knowledge of military weapons.

§

Dear Professor Elemental,

I enclose a letter from my brother, and implore you to come to his aid. I have only been able to see him for a little time. From the state of his face, I fear he has been ill-treated. Algernon has a strong mind and will not be forced into false confession, I think, nor is he the kind of man who would accuse another in order to save his own life. The police will not hear his suspicions about the Plunkett sisters; we think they have spoken with Maude, but we have no idea what has been said. Someone is making a lot of money out of killing people, and that same someone may have chosen my brother to bear the blame and the noose on their behalf. It could so easily have been yourself instead. Algernon wonders if Maude is the mind behind it all. He is convinced you are blameless but cannot give me a clear reason for this. Still, it is all we have, and these are desperate times. If we do not trust you, there is no one else we can turn to. His life is at stake.

I feel if you knew the truth about Algy, you would not hesitate to assist him, but I am sworn to secrecy. I can only beg you to help us.

Alison Spoon

§

Dear Professor,

Alison has brought me paper, but time is short. The police have your letters and Horatio's. I am accused of murdering Horatio and also of the other Hermetic and Scientific murders. They say there is evidence against me but will not say what, exactly, it is. I suspect someone has testified against me. No trial date is set. They talk of hanging me. Please get word to Maude that Horatio is safe. She should be with friends in London; hopefully he knows how to contact her. Proof that Horatio lives would help my case considerably; I can only appeal to your good will in this regard, conscious that you owe me nothing.

Whatever comes of this, I would like you to know that it was a pleasure to make your acquaintance. I would like to have known you better. You have a fine mind.

Algernon

§

Dear, Darling Alison,

Rest assured that I will do everything in my power to make sure that no one hangs me, and as a consequence I think you can trust that I will also endeavour not to see your brother suffer that grim fate. It's very decent of him not to be making this any worse for me than it already is. Tell him he's a fine chap and a true gentleman.

I've had a stiff chat with Horatio, and he's going to do the decent thing. I think having the eel in his trousers may have calmed him down a bit.

I'm quite touched by Algernon's words; it's always pleasing to be properly recognised. He's clearly a very bright fellow, with excellent taste. I find so many lesser minds unequal to the sheer scale of my genius, and it gets a bit frustrating, to say the least. As I write, I am also contemplating a rescue plan. I shan't go into details in case the police are interfering with your post at all, but suffice it to say that one can cause a great deal of mayhem with a well placed airship, and this distraction should allow good old Algy to do something fiendishly clever and get himself out of this scrape.

Sincerely,
Professor Elemental

§

Dear Professor,

Algernon says that on no account are you to crash an airship into the prison or its vicinity. The risks are too great. He thanks you for your kind thought, however, and is encouraged by your support and the hope of news from Horatio. It is his hope that after this, you and he might share a cup of tea, and he says that envisaging this keeps him from thinking too much about death.

While I am flattered by your attentions, I am not open to courtship, and where the sharing of tea is concerned, the thoroughly manly company of my brother may be the better bet. Do write to him, it would be a source of great comfort.

With thanks,
Alison Spoon

§

Lord of my dreams, I have touched your monkey. I feel so close to you now. I am sure I must have conceived and be carrying your child.

Winny

§

Dear policetrousers,

I want you to know that I am not dead. I would think my writing you this lovely letter would show that I am perfectly not dead. In my experience, dead people do not do a very good job of writing. Mostly they just lie there, and if you make them lie there for long enough, they start to emit unsavoury smells. Anyone who suggests that I emit unsavoury smells is a liar and a cad! It took us a week longer than it should have done to bury my grandmother because of the ice, you know, so I know all about what happens to dead people. She went rather squidgy, in the end.

Furthermore, having been alive for all of my life, I am quite sure I can be depended upon to have noticed should I have died, and I assure you good gentlemen of the police, that I am ~~undead~~. Ah. My friend tells me that means something that I do not mean to mean. What I wish you to understand is that I have not died in the first place, not that I died and somehow came back in a mortless condition. No! It wasn't like that at all. I am not allowed to tell you the part about Queen Victoria, but if you could only find the policeman who sang to accompany her, I am sure we could get this business sorted out. Apparently you've locked up some chap called Spoon for killing me. I'd like you to know that I only met Mister Spoon once, and we were both alive at the time, although he looked a great deal like a fox. I hope that clarifies everything,

Sincerely yours,
Horatio Plunkett

§

Dear Detective Sergeant Augustus Mentionables, Scotland Yard,

Sir, I am most grateful for the diligent efforts you have made in seeking justice for my poor brother. I received your letter this morning and am delighted to hear that the trial will be in a fortnight's time. While I should love to attend the hanging, my nerves have suffered dreadfully during this difficult period, and I am entirely unable to leave the house. I could not get through the front door even if I wanted to. I hope that my testimony would not be so important as for my absence to cause problems, because I quite literally cannot get out just now. My condition is so restricted that if anyone came to visit me, I would be unable to even go down the stairs for an interview. Most of the time, my condition does not permit me to get out of bed.

May I say again how grateful I am for your HELP and I feel sure you will RESCUE the whole nation from Spoon and the one person who will appreciate this the most is definitely ME. I hope I've made that clear enough?

Your humble, bedridden servant,
Maude Plunkett

§

Dear Horatio,

I want you to know that I am very happy with Matilda and Katherine and that everything is fine and lovely and charming, and we all sit round the piano in the evening and sing your favourite songs about horses. What a lovely time I am having. Please stay with your new chum forever and never come back. Everybody thinks you are dead. We had a charming little bonfire in the garden the other night. We burned everything that could possibly be used to prove who you are. It will be much better for both of us if you do not try to come back. Katherine and Matilda have a surprisingly large collection of military memorabilia and have promised to show me how all of it works, if the message to stay away does not come through loud and clear.

All my love,
Maude

§

Dear Professor,

I have a clever device for picking lice out of human hair. I wondered if you might like to buy it off me? I'm very cheap.

Sincerely yours,
Makepeace William Honking

§

Dear Mr Honking,

Gentlemen do not have lice, so they also do not have any need for devices to aid in the removal of them. Although if you had something for getting rid of mice, that would be far more interesting.

The working classes may have a use for your invention, but you won't get any takers there because the whole poverty thing tends to get in the way of progress. In short, yours is a rather silly idea, and I do not wish to purchase one. You should instead consider investing in the Gentleman's Pocket Grooming Set, including a small butler automata. Weighing a mere fifty pounds, it is ideal for the fellow who travels lightly and may need a good shave at any moment and doesn't mind losing some skin during the shaving process and has some kind of externally-carried blood supply for emergency consumption in case of arteries being cut by mistake.

Sincerely etc,
Professor Elemental

§

From the Diary of Algernon Spoon...

This, at least, the police did not take, and if all else fails, Alison may be able to use it in the fullness of time to clear my name posthumously. With luck and some genius on my part, it will not come to that. I have two weeks until I face trial, but the coffin maker has already been in to measure me for burial.

There seems to be no doubt that I will die for my crimes, and the papers are full of ever wilder speculation about my motives. None of them get close to the truth of who I am. Perhaps, when the final moment comes, I shall rip open my shirt and let the world see who, exactly, they have chosen to slaughter. It is tempting.

I have two weeks in which to prove my innocence. Dear, brave Alison has taken my place in prison so that I can undertake to solve the mystery of my own framing. The guards are not that attentive, and we look much alike. She has cut her beautiful hair for me, which breaks my heart. I did not used to suffer emotion a great deal, but recent events have moved me in so many ways.

Everything now depends upon the Plunkett siblings. If Maude is behind it all, then I see little hope for me. However, if it is Katherine and Matilda, or those who counterfeit them, then Maude may yet save my life. Horatio alone proves nothing. Alison tells me he has sent a letter, but with no one to identify him and no documents to his name, he is powerless. The only course of action is to see if Maude is a prisoner or a willing participant in my downfall.

I shall go to Horatio and seek his aid. He is man enough to do the right thing by his sister, even if he is a little deranged. His friendship with the Professor may secure us some assistance. My mind is awash with plans and schemes. I am better used to being the unraveller of plots than the creator, but I think I can manage this well enough.

It will be good to see the Professor again. He intrigues me, and this last week I have consoled myself by bringing our brief conversation to mind, when sleep has evaded me at night. He cuts a curious figure. If they do hang me, my chief regret, aside from the whole unpleasantness of dying, will be that I did not have the time to know him better. That, and what will become of my poor sister.

I am hardly at all myself tonight. I think of poor Alison, who now occupies my prison bed. Dear, brave girl, she says I have endured more, and she will equal me and share the burden of my suffering. Was there ever greater courage or love than this? She has tried so hard on my behalf to rally support and win my freedom. It grieves me to think of her in that dank cell, but if I die, what will become of her? As my secretary, she has a wage and independence, she has the sheltering influence of a brother. I do not doubt she is determined and clever enough to continue without me, but it will be a hard life for her, and I wanted better. And so, I try to buy her future and the expense of the present, and hope I do not fail.

Alison, if this comes to you and I am no more, I beg you to forgive me.

§

To the Editor of the Times,

I am writing to recommend Mapplethwaite teas as being far superior to any other for stimulating the creative mind. Especially if you add a drop of whatever happens to be in the laboratory at the time. It goes so very nicely with turpentine. Furthermore, if you have any dead badgers you need to soak pending unprecedented acts of experimentation, you can't beat a nice vat of Mapplethwaite tea. Any other business person wishing to see my endorsement is advised to send me lots of money and at least a sketch of what the product looks like.

Sincerely,
Professor Elemental

§

Mr Elemental,

I keep dreaming about you, and in every dream you drink my tea and tell me that it is made from the vomit of orphans. I am selling my business; you leave me with no choice. I am going to Australia to become a Nun.

Fustram Mapplethwait

§

Dear Professor Elemental,

Are you interested in shadowy plots to overthrow modern society? Have you been approached by dubious associations offering membership? Have you been miss-sold a peerage or declined a knighthood? Englebert and Horsechopper, lawyers of long standing service, are yours to command. For a reasonable fee, we will make sure that your social rating is top notch and that you get invited to all the right dinner parties again. Simply join our new, friendly society, The Brotherhood of Benevolence, and for a modest monthly donation, we will ensure that no further harm befalls you.

Sincerely yours,
Mr Horace Englebert and Mr Kevin Horsechopper

§

From the Diary of Algernon Spoon

It is strange to be dressed in my sister's clothes, living in her flat and trying to pass myself off as her. Still, I cannot go back to my own digs too often for fear of drawing attention.

NO EXPLOSIONS, NO BADGERS – JUST GOOD, WHOLESOME ENGLISH TEA!

Looking in the mirror and seeing her face more than my own is a touch uncanny. A wig makes so much difference to the way a face appears, and of course I have taken off my moustache.

I went in to my office today. It is a mess after the police 'search' and hard to tell what I have lost. Still, that can wait until larger matters are dealt with. I resisted the urge to tidy up and concentrated on the new post...

Dear Mr Spoon,

You're the chap who looks like a fox, yes? Big bushy tail, habit of running around on four legs? Do you have a sister, by any chance? I'm sure I recognise you from somewhere. Anyway, I would like you to know that I am quite clear about you not having killed me. Do show this letter anywhere it might help.

The papers say that Maude hired you, and you then stole all our money and killed all our relatives. Did Maude hire you? I'm very confused. Why would she hire you to steal all our money?

Horatio Plunkett

Dear Algernon,

Alison encouraged me to write to you. I assume some grand plan for smuggling my letters in to prison? I would have thought a weapon the more obvious choice. I know the pen is supposed to be mightier than the sword, but only if you reinforce it with steel, which makes it tricky to write with. I speak from experience in this matter.

Well, this is still rather a sorry mess, and I had hoped all would be well by now. Mr Plunkett is improving by the day, though. I am looking after him and am mostly able to keep him safely on the inside of a good pair of trousers. So, a plan to frame me, you say? And what a near miss I have had; I should hate to be in prison, all that darkness and being locked up, not to mention the company of the criminally-minded. I lost the better part of a night's sleep just imagining what might have happened to me if I hadn't been lucky enough to have been replaced by you. I suppose that puts me just a little bit in your debt, and I can't help but think that whoever did this might still be after me, and if they hang you, I doubt you'll be able to solve the thing. You do solve mysteries, yes? I suppose if you don't solve this one, that will be rather a permanent stain on your record. Tricky to solve something from inside a prison, I imagine. Even harder once you're dead. And if I were to be dead… but no, some things are far too depressing to speak of, even by letter.

I've always thought detectiving would be a rather

entertaining line of work, and I can't help but think there's a lovely ring to 'Professor Elemental, Criminal Investigator'. How does a chap get into this line of things, then? Is there a membership of some kind? I do hope not. They always turn out to be far more trouble than I'd like.

Geoffrey feels that we should undertake to heroically rescue you and is attempting to make keys out of soap. Apparently this makes for very clean locks, but I do not hold out any great hopes for it as a strategy. I've had to get out of a good few things in my time, not just wardrobes and attics, but a surprising number of outhouses, coal cellars, carriages, flying machines and several pairs of trousers that turned out to have rather an excess of free will. So far, no prisons, and on reflection I am unsure of quite how this has come to be, given the remarkable number of times I've been threatened with the very same.

If I create an army of midget soldiers, we can storm the prison and free you, carrying you to safety on the back of a clockwork elephant. That should surprise them!

What do you think?

Sincerely etc,
Professor Elemental

My prison break yesterday was a quiet, untheatrical affair. Hard to envisage the midget army. I have to get to them before they do anything rash, or make things worse. It's odd – I have read so many of the Professor's letters and elicited several under false pretences. This is the first one he has written to me. I am touched by his generosity, even though I am also aware that his motive is self-protection.

§

Beloved, why do you ignore me? I wait outside your house every day, and yet you never seem to see me. Why do you not look down, heart of my heart? Love is not measured in inches, surely? And I've been so careful to cover my teeth. What must I do to hold your heart in my hands?

Winny

§

Dear Professor Elemental,

We send you this doll's head to remind you of the fragile nature of life and the importance of safeguarding your eternal soul.

The Anglican Reformer's League

§

Professor Elemental, Note to self

Box up doll's heads and send them back to the Anglicans. Or send to the Hermetic and Scientific gentlemen in case they like that sort of thing? Risky. May take it as an insult. Must not offend them. Life may depend on it, and do not wish to spend my final moments in curious intimacy with a goat. Send doll's heads to tragic orphans? They are a bit creepy. Do orphans like creepy things, or will it remind them of the terrible deaths of their parents? Postage will cost a fortune anyway. Waste of money. Can't have them cluttering up the hall.

Further note to self: Stop bloody procrastinating and do something. See? You're still doing it. You're writing this note and the dolls are all staring at you.

My God!

The badgers!

§

Geoffrey,

Get more copper wire and at least another bucket-full of nails and more glue for fixing the china heads and a nice Battenberg cake. But this time can we not have nails or glue in the cake, or cake in the bucket, or any other configuration that does not lend itself to me ultimately eating said cake, but which instead results in you eating my cake. Can we add, no monkey hairs adhered to the cake and no signs of nibbling. Under no circumstances are you to surrender my cake to the mice, either. They've already had a whole wheel of Stilton this week.

Professor Elemental

§

Professor Elemental, Note to self

Train badger minions to hunt down and destroy enormous mice! Ha! Give mice peanuts and await the screams of death. Go, my beautiful badger minions, go!

Further note to self: Get more secure shelves to climb on for occasions of badger minion revolt. Get more peanuts. Find use for corpses of giant, partially-chewed rodents. Cancel cheese order. Consider abandoning animal experiments for something safer, like bomb-making or jumping from great heights wearing a flying machine that consists of a couple of swans' wings and some string. I do have some swans' wings, thinking about it.

Extra note to self: get more string.

WOULD BADGERS SERVE THE CAKE OR EAT IT?

UNRELIABLE BEASTS!

§

From the Diary of Algernon Spoon...

I feel so naked in women's attire. No matter how many layers and petticoats there are, none of it is as reassuring as a stout pair of trousers. I took a small travelling case so as to look like a poor but respectable woman making a perfectly reasonable journey. A woman without a bag or a servant of some kind immediately creates suspicion. The bag, however, allowed me to carry some trousers – and the promise of returning to my more usual self.

Arriving at the gates of the Professor's house, I immediately scanned my surroundings for signs of possible discovery. All appeared quiet. The only figure in sight was a midget woman apparently selling lemonade by the glass. I approached her. My mind raced with possibilities, and so I approached her, as nonchalantly as possible.

"I'd like a glass, please."

"What?" she stared up at me, horse-featured and full of resentment.

"A glass of lemonade, please," I repeated, trying hard not to smirk.

"Haven't got any."

"Your sign clearly states otherwise."

She looked around desperately. "There was a big mail coach, you just missed it, lots of thirsty people riding up top. All sold out now."

"And they even bought the glasses," I could not resist observing.

She stared harder, eyes bulging slightly. "What do you want?"

"You're Winifred, aren't you?"

She gaped, her parted lips revealing the most unsightly teeth it has ever been my misfortune to behold. "Who are you?"

It was my turn to smile. "My grandmother was a gypsy, and I have inherited the second sight," I improvised.

"Can you do futures?" she asked hopefully.

I took her greasy palm. "The man you love does not notice you, but I see another future awaiting you, many miles from here. A bright and happy future, in Doncaster!"

She pouted. "That can't be right."

I had tried to spare her from pain and reassured myself that my motives were good. Hardly able to enter the front gates with the mad and obsessive Winifred watching me, I carried on down the road. As anticipated, the grandeur of the frontage soon gave way to a much more regular, and easily penetrated, hedge.

§

Dear Gentlemen of Hay-in-the-Marsh Parish Council,

My wife and I moved to Hay-in-the-Marsh last summer, after my having retired from a long and illustrious career in the civil service, where I was Privy to the Queen's Chamber for some years. We took on a modest property to this unremarkable village of yours, seeking the peace of the countryside and opportunities to chase wild creatures with dogs, and to shoot peasants.

We are sorely disappointed by the quality of noble personages in the parish and wish to protest that we have been lured here under false pretences. We were assured of a gentile society in which to spend our twilight years. But no, Hay-in-the-Marsh instead graces us with banging, night and day. Not the elevated banging of rich people shooting the wildlife, but the horrible sound of cottage industry. I say 'cottage' but the varlet has the largest property for miles around. I allude to Professor Elemental and his monstrous constructions. He is not an appropriate person for this locality, and I hereby request that you have him removed to some grubby little northern industrial town where his perpetual hammering will not cause offence to more refined ears.

In good faith,
Ackrington Overture BA,
MBE, EJO, BBC

§

Badger Minion Army Experimentation Notes

Badger minions now effectively trained in forward samba formation, the stealth foxtrot and an entirely malicious form of tango. And to think everyone said exotic dancing would never be of any use to a real man! Ah, how my creations polka! Next we shall work on a move of my own devising, called 'gnaw the enemy's face off'. Less popular in my dancing partner automata, but rather charming in a trained minion, I feel.

§

From the Diary of Algernon Spoon...

The lawn was not as I remembered it. Vast, metallic constructions dominated the grounds before the main building. Sounds of banging, punctuated by uncouth language, floated intermittently on the breeze.

"That's never going to work, Geoffrey, you fool," shouted a now familiar voice.

As I came closer, I also spotted Horatio Plunkett, decently

trousered and waving a hammer. "You should re-invent the wheel," he was saying. "Bloody sight faster, wheels."

"Wheels belong to history," the Professor replied. "Ancient savages had wheels. Where's your sense of adventure, man?"

"Well damn me, Professor, there's a filly on the lawn and a fine one at that!" Plunkett observed.

I had no plan as to how I would present myself, skirted as I was. The Professor descended from his strange contraption and looked me over. "That's not a filly, Plunkett, you idiot, that's Mr Spoon dressed in his sister's clothes. I recognise the chin. And the eyes, come to that."

"You're a perceptive man, Professor," I said, using my Algernon voice rather than the Alison voice the skirt had necessitated.

"Makes a fine woman though," Plunkett added. "Now, that's what I need, some kind of ladyboy, talks like a chap, thinks like a chap, moves like a filly."

I caught the Professor's eye and could see the direction his mind had taken. For a happy moment we were co-conspirators.

"There are clubs for that sort of thing," he said. "Never been in anything like it myself, of course, apart from that one time, but I was running away from a rather angry mob, and that makes a considerable difference."

"Extreme situations call for extreme measures," I said, gesturing towards the skirt.

"You don't make a bad girl, though," he said. "Amazing

what a corset and an old pair of socks can do, eh?" He squeezed me in a location that, had he assumed me to be female, would have been rather shocking. As it was, I felt quite seriously shocked, never having been squeezed in quite that way before.

"We're about ready to roll," Horatio pronounced. "We were coming to rescue you."

I took this opening to try and redirect the mayhem towards my own vision of a way forwards. "I think we need to rescue Maude instead," I suggested.

"She's at home," Plunkett replied. "That would seem a bit redundant."

"Katherine and Matilda are not really your sisters," I explained.

"Are you casting aspersions on my mother?" Plunkett demanded, face red with fury. "She was a fine and virtuous woman, and I will not have her spoken about as though she was some sort of… some kind of… that which we will not speak of in front of the ape."

I took a cautious step back, out of punching range. "When did you last see either Katherine or Matilda without a veil?"

He frowned. "Been a while," he said.

"That would explain a great deal. There are two criminal men, who are at this very moment masquerading as two of your sisters and holding the third one prisoner, I think," I said.

"Of course if this is wrong and we roll in and Maude

doesn't need rescuing..." the Professor began.

"Then at least we shall know she is safe. If she knows Horatio is safe, I may be able to get the murder charge dropped, leaving me with the task of swapping places with my sister."

"Ah, that old trick," Elemental observed. "Looks like you, I take it?"

"Identical twin," I replied, too caught up in the moment to properly guard my tongue. If he noticed the slip, he said nothing.

I realise that this whole experience has unhinged my emotions somewhat and that my capacity for calmness and self control are sorely impaired. I must make the best of it and endeavour not to kill anybody. Or at least, not to kill anyone where I cannot easily prove self-defence.

§

Professor Elemental, Note to self

Do not spend time with badgermingos, badger minions or anything else stripy and badger-shaped when feeling the lack of female companionship. However rounded their rumps may be, however soft their fur, a man can go too far, and I fear the bites may turn septic.

If only Maude hadn't refused my advances. Curse that

Goddingford fellow. I'm sure it was all his fault. If only sweet Appolina hadn't turned out to be a demented ex-butler in drag. If only Algernon were really a girl and not just in disguise. He makes a very fine girl. It's one thing offering your love trousers to a chap in a dress who you really don't think is a chap in a dress, and quite another when you think you do know. Would that be worse than badgers? If only Geoffrey were a woman in disguise. Although I suppose he could be a she-ape; it's not as if I've ever checked closely… but there was that business with the female ape pictures. That would make Geoffrey an ape of Lesbos, and frankly that wouldn't help me even a little bit.

If only the woman stalking me looked half as attractive as my lovely badgers, but her lack of symmetry troubles me far too much. Apparently I still have some standards. Not many though. Fewer by the day, in fact.

There must, surely, be some attractive, adventuresome girl out there who has all her own teeth, a full complement of sanity, an inheritance, a keen appreciation of my talents, a desire to worship me and a figure that looks good in a boiler suit. Is that really too much to ask? And stripy hair. Like a badger. And lots of gin.

Ah well, I've got some gin, even if it doesn't want to see my love trousers. Dear, kind, forgiving gin. If only you had a lot of money and some breasts.

§

Dear world,

Please be quieter. I am having quite enough trouble with the evil dwarfs who are practicing drum rolls inside my head, badly. You spiders do not need to join in by donning little iron shoes before you run across the floorboards. Mice? I ascribe you to the gin. You do not exist. Go away.

Sincerely,
Professor Elemental

§

Dear Professor, Mwahahahahahhaha.
Love, the unkillable mice.
PS. We ate the crotch out of your love trousers.

§

Signs of the End Times

As we draw closer to the end of the century, many of us ask: is the second coming of Jesus fast approaching? Will we see the events described in Revelations unfold before our very eyes? Many of us believe it to be so. Last night, I witnessed an event so powerful and frightening in its magnitude that I feel certain it is a harbinger of the day of judgement.

With monstrous clanking and unearthly sounds, I saw a fiend from the pit pass across our innocent countryside, its eyes blazing, maniacal laughter come from its vile innards. Even now the thought fills me with a numinous kind of dread.

I know certain personages have disparaged my judgement before, but I wish to assure you that I was entirely sober at the time of the observation, and all that I witnessed can be vouched for by the two choirboys who were with me at the time, discussing matters of faith and suchlike.

Your humble servant,
The Reverend Amiable Gundersludge

§

I stood on a box today and it didn't help me a little bit. You didn't even seem to notice the squirrel in my hair. What kind of man are you? Are you the other sort? One of the ones who does unmentionable things to the wrong side of their toast? Surely, a man with such perfect knees could not be so depraved as that? So depraved as to prefer wrong toast to the love of a short and only slightly horse-faced woman who wants to have your babies and who has already sacrificed her virtue for you. What a total bastard you are.

Winny

§

From the Diary of Algernon Spoon...

I am writing this as a way to control my thoughts about all that is happening around me right now. The act of applying pen to paper is extremely difficult, and I am wearing a good deal more ink that I consider seemly, but, God help me, staring at this page is a lot less disturbing than looking up, in any direction. I am inside Professor Elemental's flying machine. The same machine that has crashed several times in the vicinity of Ipswich. I can only hope the marks on the floor are not blood stains. Mercifully, we are not flying. I might not have dared to make the journey airborne. Instead, we lurch alarmingly, in an unholy amalgam of airship, giant robot and midget army.

I have no idea how any of this is working. I have furthermore come to the conclusion that it is probably better not to know. My three travelling companions are continually hitting, tightening, loosening and otherwise modifying that which surrounds us. Their words are as incoherent to me as a foreign language. I am terrified to the core of my unfortunate being. Perhaps hanging would have been less traumatic. I am sure I ought to have died several times now. This is madness, or hell, or both. We lurch, stumble, crash and somehow, against all odds and reason, we continue. Each time the whole apparatus collapses to the ground, I am thrown about violently, the ink spills, Elemental shouts at Geoffrey, steam sprays us, something explodes, and yet somehow we do not die.

Dear sweet God, Jesus, Mary, mother of toast MAKE IT STOP!

I can see why the gentlemen are so partial to laudanum. I have been given to understand that it soothes the nerves. I should rather like a whiskey, at the very least. About a pint, for preference.

If this is the shape of the future, I am very worried. I can only hope not much more of my future involves being tossed about like this. I may be going to throw up. Or pass out. Possibly both. This may be humiliating. I don't want to die. I think it would be better to die than to arrive at our destination shaking, incoherent and covered in my own vomit. As rescue missions go, that would lack something for style. At least I still have my infamous wit with which to protect myself.

§

Dear whoever finds this bat,

I am being kept prisoner in my own home. It is part of a complicated plot, and I am unsure who is responsible. Please inform the police. Although I consider myself to be an independent woman, I could rather do with rescuing. Also, the bat I tied this to is a little bit tame and would probably like a moth now. With thanks in advance for your kind assistance,

Maude Plunkett,
Plunkett Villa

§

Dear Professor Elemental,

I'd like to book all of my elderly relatives for a lovely day out to Ipswich in your remarkable flying machine. Would it be convenient if I were to pay for the tickets after the funerals?

Many thanks,
Norman Elephant

§

From the Diary of Algernon Spoon...

Oh God, if I die inside this monstrous machinery, Alison will be hanged in my stead. If I have died and anyone finds this, please try to save her. Scotland Yard have mistakenly imprisoned Alison Spoon, not Algernon Spoon; the slightest attempt at a medical examination should reveal the truth.

I look back at my recent ramblings with some feelings of embarrassment. The following I compose with a calmer head and far fewer vibrations, explosion and sudden life-threatening plummets… It is also written somewhat after the events I am about to describe…

Finally, the infernal contraption came to a halt, and we crashed only slightly. The absence of noise was a joy to my abused ears, but we had no time to waste.

"Geoffrey can climb up and rescue her. He got me out that way," Plunkett suggested.

The monkey butler seemed keen to enact the plan at once, replacing his white shirt with darker attire.

"How did you actually leave, Mister Plunkett?" I enquired.

"Oh, first names, my dear foxy-faced fellow. Call me Horatio! Or Lovepuppy, if you prefer."

It took a moment to steer him back to the issue at hand, but eventually he stopped thinking about chasing fox tails and focused his laudanum-addled mind.

"I dangled the sheets out of the window, to cause confusion, then went downstairs and let myself out through the kitchen door. After that, it was easy. Apart from the bit with the angry weasels."

"I do not think it will be as easy to extract Maude. They will have made some provisions to prevent her from leaving."

I scanned the dark bulk of the Plunkett mansion, looking for inspiration. It struck almost at once. There, away to the right, almost obscured by the trees behind it, was a most un-house-like shape. "Is that not the famous water-slide?" I asked.

"Indeed it is," Plunkett said. "It doesn't quite go to the centre of the earth, although I understand it does cause your digestive system to assume that precisely such a journey has been made."

"What were you thinking of doing with my masterpiece?" the Professor asked, his tone suspicious.

"Climbing up it," I at once replied.

"It wasn't designed for that. I can take no responsibility for what it does, if you insist on going up it," he said.

"Is it likely to be dangerous?" I enquired of him.

"Well… I suppose that depends a good deal on your precise definition of 'dangerous'. But probably, yes. But there won't be any splinters. I was exceedingly careful in that regard. I did, however, end up reusing one or two things from another project…"

"Yes?"

"Well, none of the poisonous bits, obviously, and I took all the spikes off first. At least, I told Geoffrey to take all the spikes off. And the razor wire. I'm sure you'll be perfectly fine."

"You aren't volunteering to go first, then?" I couldn't resist asking.

"You'll need someone to guard the base, in case anyone comes along with pointed sticks, or dogs, or fruit, or a gramophone with a particularly offensive musical recording on it. That could alarm you into losing your balance." He looked around. "Also, the midget army are trying to take over the gazebo; I really feel it's my moral duty to make sure they don't entirely destroy the garden."

We left him trying to wrestle one of the small creatures off a statue. I am unsure whether they were machine or animal in origin, or some alarming combination of the two. The near-darkness was a blessing in this regard.

The wood of the water-slide had been smoothed to perfection and took some climbing. Geoffrey made good speed, but then, being able to hang on with four hands effectively conveys a distinct advantage. On reaching the first corner, we found a large, brightly-painted rendition of the Professor's face, and from his nose came one of the 'sharp things' he had previously alluded to. Any wrong move on this slide could easily lead to death, or at least the loss of a limb.

"You know, I've not slid down this yet," Horatio announced. "I meant to. Even without the water running, it is lovely." We watched him slide away, laughing like an insane child. I could only hope that our adversaries were too occupied with songs of Frenchmen and horses to notice our unsubtle approach.

Twice I slipped, and only Geoffrey's fast reflexes saved me from the perilous fall. At last, we made the summit, a mere ten feet or so from the roof of the house. My primate companion leapt easily across. I surveyed the distance, less confident in my jumping prowess.

"Problems?" the Professor stage-whispered up from the gloom.

"Bit of a gap," I said.

"I'll send up a couple of midgets. Hang on."

I waited, listening to the slithering sounds of what I could only hope was approaching assistance. In no time at all, the midgets clung together, creating a living bridge between waterslide and roof. I walked across them, and they uttered not one sound of protest. Thank goodness the dark obscured the fall, for I think, had I been able to see, I should not have had the courage to make so perilous a crossing.

We found an attic window, and Geoffrey had us in with amazing speed. Armed with a good working knowledge of the house, I made all haste for Maude's room. Outside, Horatio gave the happy shriek of a man who has descended a dry water-slide and successfully avoided all the sharp and pointy bits.

We hurried as quietly as we could towards Maude's rooms but arrived too late. Three figures stood at the open window. My client, Maude, held firm between two broad men, their stubble-encrusted faces a sorry contrast to the lacy dresses both wore. Matilda and Katherine were indeed Murkin and…

I recognised the other man: John the Retriever, the floating sage of Covent Garden. In turn I saw that he recognised me.

"I warned you, Spoon, not to go messing in the business of true mages," he said.

With that, he turned, and, before I could intervene, the

two men leapt from the window, carrying Maude between them. I heard her scream of "Idiots!" rising up on the air and waited for the fatal crash, but none came. Apparently the floating mystic had enough power for passengers. It all made sense – the hiding, the wax cylinders. The dastardly pair could come and go as they pleased, floating in and out of the window without anyone else suspecting a thing! My God! I would never have dared to image so audacious a plan as this.

I had little time to reflect upon the brilliance of their scheme, though. Already the most troubling sounds were rising from the garden. Geoffrey and I rushed to the window in time to see an awkward landing. The additional weight of Maude's buxom figure was apparently more than the mystic could bear. At once, the Professor rushed towards them, clearly intent on slowing them down. I couldn't hear the initial exchange, but fists were raised.

"Queensbury rules!" called out the Professor, dancing nimbly from one foot to the other in a manner clearly designed to confuse the opponent. His attention was focused on Murkin.

"Behind you!" I shouted, but in vain, for the floating mystic made a most un-gentlemanly approach, grasped the Professor on his shoulder, and felled him with a single move. It was uncanny, the way he slumped onto the grass. Geoffrey took this as his cue to climb from the window and make a hurried descent. There was nothing I could do. They dragged Maude into the darkness, and I watched in horror as the half-finished midget army trundled obediently behind them. We had failed, spectacularly.

§

To Detective Sergeant Augustus Mentionables, Scotland Yard,

I was called to the scene of the crime a little after dawn, alerted by servants from the house. We don't get a lot of crime round here; it's mostly the occasional theft of cows, the odd speeding bicycle, and Dr Moffat's little trouser problem. I'm not saying my boys are green and inexperienced, but the destruction of certain pieces of evidence – most especially the unfortunate burning of the water-slide, the failure to locate Maude Plunkett, and the reckless stampede cross-county that wrecked any hope of picking up the trail with dogs, should not be judged too harshly, I implore. They are good lads, just a bit out of their depth.

We discovered a gentleman on the lawn who claims to be Horatio Plunkett. Servants from the house were able to support this assertion, so we are working on the assumption that he is who he claims to be. The three sisters Maude, Katherine and Matilda Plunkett are all missing. We had a confusing statement from Mr Plunkett in which he said that Maude had been kidnapped, and that Katherine and Matilda were really men and the thing with the horses was all a cunning ruse. I'm not sure what this means. When asked if his sisters had always been men, he admitted to not knowing.

According to Mr Plunkett, the absolute destruction of his garden, a nearby pig farm and several trees was due to the following: Professor Elemental's midget army, which ran away. Professor Elemental's airship, which doesn't fly so much as hops along the ground, breaking things. Professor Elemental's giant robot version of himself, which is currently being steered by a monkey butler called Geoffrey. We asked Mr Plunkett if he had imbibed any mind-altering substances. He said, 'Yes, I know, thank you very much, that's why I left out the bit about the fish ballet and the chap who is secretly a fox. Don't try to tell me I have no idea what's real."

Based on this evidence, we are now conducting a house-to-house search for Professor Elemental, as he's the only one we've got a name for and enough evidence to arrest. In the meantime, you might want to look into the kidnapping angle.

Sincerely yours,
Amanuel Kant Skippingly
Chief of Police for the Parish of Slaughtering Bottom

§

Beloved, you do not have to marry me; I will be your slave, your woman of ill-repute, your floozy. But please, let me touch those magnificent knees with my un-gloved hands. I don't care what kind of bastard you are, I forgive you. Perhaps I could rub cod liver oil onto your legs? Is there anything in the world more alluring than the smell of a fishy knee? I am fainting with rapture at the mere thought of it.

Winny

§

From the Diary of Algernon Spoon…

Geoffrey roused the good professor from unconsciousness by the simple expedient of slapping him about the face with a wet cloth.

"Those evil, heartless, scheming, manipulative bastards!" were his words upon waking. He seemed genuinely distressed. "How did they know? Damn them all to the darkest, most bug-infested pits of hell!"

I ventured to ask what on earth he was talking about.

His movements became dramatic, and I stepped back to avoid the ever-more expansive gestures. "They had groundnuts. My midget army was powerless to resist! They've forsaken me, lured away by the delights of a nut that isn't even a proper nut by any decent, scientific measure. Fickle beasts."

"You may not be aware that the man accompanying Eddie

210 • *Letters Between Gentlemen*

Asparagus Murkin was none other than John the Retriever, the floating mystic of Covent Garden. It may be that he has psychic powers as well as the floating."

"And thus knew how to seduce my cunningly-crafted midget army," the professor snarled. "Well, he'll be in trouble when the peanuts run out, I can tell you."

"They have Maude and your midgets. We must go after them," I pronounced, even though I knew with awful dread what that must mean.

We took to the airship.

"It's all about the wind," Professor Elemental told me as we catapulted ourselves erratically from one tree to another. "And the not crashing too hard into the ground. That makes a lot of odds." I could see Geoffrey behind us at the controls of the giant robot. Without the midget army holding it all together, we'd become two death-defying contraptions, rather than one.

"It's easy to see where they went, dear creatures that they are," the Professor observed, pointing out a clear track of total destruction. Once we reached the road, the hedge carnage made it easy enough to keep up pursuit.

"What are they?" I asked, thinking it likely that the horror of the midgets would distract me a bit from the even bigger horror of our bone-shaking progress.

"Well, I had a lot of spare badger bodies lying about, from the badgermingo project, and it seemed a pity to waste them. I started by fitting them up with dolls' heads. I find it helps to have a face I can talk to; I'm sure you understand. Then, rather a lot of wiring, extra teeth. To be honest I'm not quite sure how they eat, with the dolls' heads, but they do, and often in great quantities. In fact, they're rather indiscriminate. Murkin and the floating chap will be fine while the peanuts last, but beyond that… let's just say that as awful ways to die go, being eaten by the midget army at least has the merits of being fairly quick. Based on what happened at the school picnic that I took them to."

"We're heading for London," I said, spotting the reassuring gloom of proper smog on the horizon. "I wonder what they're planning?"

"Well at a guess, the public murder of Maude, in a way that implicates you as ringleader of the Hermetic and Scientific gentlemen. This will then cause a riot, screaming, death, all the usual, an assault on the Houses of Parliament is a given, the midgets will be unleashed, and by the end of the day Murkin will have claimed power and London will have been swallowed entirely by a giant tidal wave coming up the river."

"How do you know all this?" I asked, incredulous.

He shrugged. "It's an informed guess. Or at least, it's what I'd do if I'd stolen a midget army and was trying to get a lot of people into a great deal of trouble at short notice. It's as well for the world that I've always been determined to use my genius for good and not for evil."

As he spoke, the airship skimmed the roof off a forlorn building. From the sounds of youthful screams and weeping that followed in our wake, I rather suspected it might have been an orphanage.

§

Dear whoever finds this letter,

Please excuse the unladylike quality of my handwriting, but I write this in near darkness, inside a moving carriage and in peril not conducive to producing a fair hand. Therefore I beg that you do not judge me by the inferior formation of my letters. It is my belief that I am being taken to London by two scoundrels who have, until recently, been passing themselves off as my sisters. They are still wearing the dresses, and I rather hope they've put the veils back on because that's far less troubling. The carriage is not being pulled by horses, but by small monsters with the most disturbing heads. Several of them have tried to bite me. I am forming this letter into a paper dart in the hopes that I can fling it clear of their attentions. Please help me. I should be very easy to spot. I am the woman inside the carriage that is being towed along by diminutive horrors.

Thank you,
Maude Plunkett

§

From the Diary of Algernon Spoon...

We chased them through the night, across the remote wilderness that anywhere-outside-of-London always seems to be. The emptiness of it all would have been almost unbearable had I not been struggling continuously against the very real fear of imminent and painful death. The good Professor seemed entirely untroubled by the process of our journey. We climbed short distances into the sky, only to fall, bounce and roll our way after our quarry. The Professor must have nerves of steel and seemed to find the whole business rather amusing. I fear there may be bruises upon my bruises and there were occasions when I did not keep up my manly demeanour to the very best effect. At the time, I thought he was being very polite in not noticing, but with the advantage of hindsight, I think he in fact just didn't notice.

Somewhere on the outskirts of the city, we lost sight of Geoffrey.

"Fool of an ape," the Professor cursed. "No doubt he's been distracted by a tree that looked ever-so-slightly like a female ape. Or by fruit. Or some other entirely frivolous thing irrelevant to the very important issue of keeping me alive. Us alive. Maude alive. Yes. That. All of the above. I advise you not to employ butlers at all; in my experience they're more trouble than they're worth."

"I've a landlady, but no butler," I confessed.

"Can she cook?" he enquired.

"Passably."

"Does she make inhuman noises at odd hours of the night?"

"Only on Fridays when she has her gin," I said. He had a remarkable power to lift my spirits.

"Well then, a vast improvement on butlers; I think we have that quite clear."

From the noises ahead, it seemed that Murkin may have run out of peanuts. We climbed from the flying machine, not daring to lope our way through the capital, where people were likely to notice the damage our passing caused and involve the law in pursuing us. My legs were unsteady, but I have never felt more grateful for the firm solidity of a dirty, London street.

"Just need to round up my minions, and we can sort out Murkin and this floating chap, yes?"

I was about to ask how we should achieve any of these noble aims when Professor Elemental drew a complicated device from inside his jacket and blew into it. The resulting note was shrill.

"Oh, no, that won't do – that's for the badgermingos." He tried another, more wheezing note. "Kitten tortoise, no…" By this time a good number of local dogs had been drawn to us, and even now cocked their ears and watched with confusion painted clearly on their furry faces. When several more calls failed to elicit a response, he resorted to shouting.

"Oi, you ungrateful badger things. Come here when I whistle! Anyone would think you hadn't been trained. No, wait a minute. What did I train you to do? This is the trouble with having too many ideas. Were you supposed to kill on command, or were you the ones doing the amusing things with sticks?"

We watched as the badger-based midgets loped towards us. One of them appeared to be eating a cat. Another had a stick but did not look especially amusing.

"Back to the airship?" I asked, nervously.

"Oh no, these are my badger minions. Midget army, halt!"

Against all the odds, they stopped moving.

"I think you'll find this is my midget army now," John the Retriever said. He came up behind them, floating cross-legged a few feet above head-height.

"What have you done with Maude?" Professor Elemental demanded.

John the Retriever smiled. "The public murder of Maude, in a way that implicates you both as ringleaders of the Hermetic and Scientific gentlemen, will then cause a riot, screaming, death, all the usual, an assault on the Houses of Parliament is a given, these midgets will be unleashed, and by the end of the day Murkin will have claimed power, and London will have been swallowed entirely by a giant tidal wave coming up the river."

"Amazing," said the Professor. "It's just as I thought. How

are you doing the tidal wave?"

"The cumulative rage of the true magi of London should be sufficient to cause that. But next, Professor, I mean to have you savaged by your own creations. Not killed outright, yet, just seriously dismembered."

I saw movement behind the mystic as a large and familiar form lurched into view. If I could just buy us time, we might yet be spared. Fearful of the floating mystic's possible psychic powers, I concentrated on envisaging myself running away, screaming. It wasn't a difficult thought to hold, given the circumstances.

"I will protect you," I shouted and leapt in front of the Professor.

"Hang on there, old chap, these are my subverted minions; if anyone's going to be chewed unpleasantly, I think it ought to be me." Evidently, he too had seen the approaching figure and understood the cunning nature of my plan.

"I shall fight you for the privilege!" I took a swing at him.

"Well, this is amusing," John the Retriever said. "I could just stand here all day watching you two idiots punching each other."

"Come down here, and I'll show you my other trousers!" the Professor roared, clearly in fighting spirits now.

John the Retriever hovered almost within reach of us. "I shall enjoy listening to you scream," he said. "Badger minions, attack!"

They leapt for us.

It is a curious experience, being bitten by something that appears to have a china doll's head. I do not know what they were biting with, only that it was very sharp. Behind me, the Professor flailed and shouted, demanding allegiance from his badger creations. Above, John the Retriever laughed, but he did not laugh for long.

"I am Professor Elemental and you, the good people of Norwich…" boomed the giant robot as it brought one enormous foot down upon the floating sage's head. Apparently there are limits to the mystical aptitude for floating, and Geoffrey found them.

Hearing that greatly amplified Professor voice, the badger minions came at once to their senses and stopped trying to kill us.

"That was a bit slow, Geoffrey. What were you doing? Pausing for breakfast, perhaps?"

The monkey butler dropped to the ground, evidently pleased with himself – and with good reason. John the Retriever's still levitating legs twitched upwards from beneath one giant foot. He wouldn't be floating anywhere for a while.

Then the Professor glanced my way, and his eyes widened. "I don't want to worry you, sir, but they've done something deeply unnatural to your chest."

I'd been trying to brazen it out, but the attack on my clothing had been thorough. "It wasn't your badgers. It's a medical condition," I said quickly. "Not contagious at all. Might I borrow your jacket?"

"Good stuff. For a worrying moment there I thought you might be a girl. Thought you might have been Alison Spoon all along. You're an odd fellow, Spoon."

He relinquished his jacket, and I buttoned it over my chest, hiding the evidence.

"Please don't tell anyone," I said. "No one would hire me if they thought… well, you know. No one takes women seriously."

"I do," he said. "When they let me, which, frequently, they don't."

"We need to find Maude," I said. "She's still in danger."

§

Dear whoever finds this note,

Please help me. I am trapped inside a carriage. The odds are you have seen this carriage because I am only able to push notes out through a crack under the door, so it's probably the nearest carriage you can see as you read this. It is a mystery to me what so much paper and ink are doing in here. Please release me from this carriage or summon the police to assist me. I assure you that I am a sane gentlewoman and in no way responsible for my condition. Thank you.

Maude Plunkett

§

Dear Maude Plunkett,

Amusing though your letters are, I feel it is only fair to mention that you are passing them to me, your dear sister Katherine, and that I have no intention of letting you out of the carriage alive. Do please try to behave in a calm and ladylike fashion as you prepare to meet your maker. You may wish to take this opportunity to pray. Don't worry about what's going to happen; it should all be fairly quick and painless, especially if you remember to inhale the smoke fumes. The odds are good, that way, of your passing out and not being at all aware of the burning-to-death part of the proceedings.

We've only chosen a very select few to deliberately murder at this time, so we hope you recognise the inherent honour and are not too disappointed by the way in which this is likely to limit your future social engagements. On the plus side, you are destined to become famous, which should give you some consolation. Enjoy your death!

Your ever-loving sister,
Katherine

§

From the Diary of Algernon Spoon...

Leaving the badger minions to guard the giant robot and the mortal remains of John the Retriever, we three raced onwards in search of Maude. I say 'raced', but it was more of a brisk trot with occasional staggering. There's nothing like running down a London street with a man devoid of a jacket, and with a monkey butler, to attract curiosity. We weren't moving fast enough to be obviously criminal, and so we acquired a following. And of course once it looks like a number of people are going somewhere with enthusiasm, other people join in, just in case there turns out to be a really good queue at the end of the thing and some free cake.

I'd rather assumed they would take Maude to some iconic London location, in order to add drama and the easy recognition factor to their crime. Why merely murder a woman, when you can, for example, do it on the steps of St Paul's Cathedral? Especially if your intention is to cause fear and rioting. I'd been trying to imagine which location I'd pick if it was my evil plan.

"Where would they go?" I shouted at the Professor.

"Over there, would be my guess." He pointed. Uncannily, he had it all figured out. If I'd had more time, I might have wondered if he was somehow in on the whole thing.

They had stopped where a wheel came off the carriage. It

squatted, broken and melancholy in the middle of the street. However, a banner had been erected over it, saying "Hermetic and Scientific Gentleman of London, first annual tea party." A hooded figured was painting symbols onto the road around the carriage, and the air smelled ominously of paraffin. I noticed that a number of straw bales had been brought to the scene – most likely on the carriage roof. They now sat underneath the stationary contraption. No doubt they had been soaked in the flammable liquid. This must be why the badger minions were no longer providing the motion.

As we approached, the hooded figure straightened and pulled a packet of matches from inside his coat. "Take one step closer here, and we toast the dame," he said.

"I'm sorry, I only speak English," the Professor replied. "I have no idea what you're saying."

"Get any closer, and I'll set fire to everything, including Maude Plunkett," the hooded man repeated, clearly irritated.

"Oh, I see, you've got her locked in there, and you're going to burn her," the Professor said. "That's not very memorable, as evil plans go. There should have been a very tall building in the mix, at any rate. I'd have done it in the middle of Tower Bridge, had it been my plan. More visible. More drama. Where's your sense of occasion?" he demanded.

"Wheel came off," the man beneath the hood said. I assumed it must be Murkin.

"So I see," the Professor said, stroking his chin. "Well, all we need to do is get enough people round it and we can wheel it the rest of the way. This lot should do. Who wants to help set fire to something?"

There were enough apprentices in the crowd and sufficiently few people who understood what was happening. We got the straw back on the roof, and the banner down, then started pushing.

"What on earth is your plan?" I asked the Professor, when Murkin was out of earshot.

"No idea," he said. "Buying time. Which has worked for now."

"Yes, but at some point we'll get to Tower Bridge. Then what?"

"We'll improvise. Wildly. Mind you, in all fairness, it'll be your turn to have a good idea at that point."

"Thank you very much."

I considered the carriage. Climb underneath and make a hole in the bottom? Not too dangerous at this speed. Take a long route through every back street in the hope of being stopped?

"Got it," I said. I told him the plan.

"That's pure lunacy," he replied.

I gave back his jacket, which was tricky, given the press of people moving the carriage. Then, with chest somewhat exposed, I made a very slow run for it.

"My god!" the Professor shouted from behind me. "She's getting away! Stop her!"

I turned, making sure everyone got a good look at my exposed chest, and then, having drawn their attention, I ran like a madwoman, arms clenched across the revealing, and revealed flesh. The crowd ran after me. I could only hope Murkin would be with them. And that I could run fast enough. And that the Professor would manage to save Maude.

§

To the Editor of The Times,

Why, why do the paupers of today spend so much time on pointless activity when they could be working hard and making money? Do they not understand that by working fourteen-hour days, six days a week, and saving diligently, they might hope to avoid debt, if not actually elevate themselves from abjection? And yet they insist on squandering their pennies on gin and tobacco and other such vices. Only this morning I saw a whole group of paupers milling about in the street, not one of them gainfully employed. They were all talking enthusiastically, and when I stopped to suggest they might be better off getting themselves into factories, I was publically scorned and insulted! I fear that moral standards are decaying, if such demonstrations of disrespect to their betters are becoming normal.

Sincerely,
Henry Obstreperous Skankponder
of the International Gin and Tobacco Company

§

From the Diary of Algernon Spoon…

It was a tricky business, losing the mob whilst keeping Murkin on my tail. The absence of a night's sleep and the shredding of my nerves by the flying machine did not leave me at my best, and my one thought was to end this, and quickly. At least, having fled through the night in a carriage pulled by rewired badgers, the probability was that Murkin had little more energy and composure left than I did.

I turned down a narrow alleyway and realised at once I had hit a dead end. Tall, grim-looking buildings gazed down at me from either side. There were no obvious ways out, and I did not think I could run any further. I turned to face my foe.

Murkin had a knife, which he made sure I could see.

"You aren't Maude Plunkett. You're that Spoon fellow. No, you're the Spoon girl, the secretary, yes?"

I nodded, still too winded from the run to try to speak. Better people assumed me to be Alison, although she might not thank me for the exposure.

"Well, you aren't what I had in mind, but you'll make a

charming corpse, and I'll be sure to arrange you in an amusing way." He stepped forward.

Murkin held his knife like a man who expects that the knife itself will cause fear. He had too tight a grip on the handle, and it was a little too far in front of him. His was not the stance of a street brawler. Whatever else had underpinned his famous criminal career, Eddie 'Asparagus' Murkin had not carved out his name with a short blade.

I let him come to me, watching him move while my body calmed from the recent exertion.

"You can scream for mercy if you like, girly. I do enjoy a good screamer."

I said nothing.

"Pity we don't have time to do a nice, slow, thorough job of you."

I lunged, my left hand grasping for his knife hand. Murkin pulled back the arm, fast enough that I couldn't grab him. But he'd made the most fundamental mistake. He'd paid too much attention to the knife and not kept an eye on my right hand. I thumped him in the gut. Then it all got very up close and personal, with my knee finding his groin, as I went again for the knife. The thing about bringing a knife to a fight is that, if you are not a knife-fighting expert, and the other person is, what you've effectively done is arm them. It's also the case, I have noticed with interest on more than one occasion, that incompetent knife-fighters tend to be tense in the arms.

Murkin still had his fingers wrapped around the knife hilt when I turned the blade back on him. I saw the look of disbelief on his face as the blade went in. What a good job he'd sharpened it so carefully! There was hardly any resistance at all. Of course a clean cut to the stomach can be rather slow in terms of killing, so I turned his hand, and the blade with it. Uttering one final, dismayed grunt, Murkin went down.

I was still gasping for breath and standing over his corpse when a third figure entered the scene. I knew I wouldn't have any trouble pleading self-defence. That's one of the joys of keeping the knife in the other man's hand as you kill him with it. Sweat made my vision hazy and I had to blink a few times before I realised who had found me.

"You took some keeping up with," said Professor Elemental. He strolled over, looking as cool as the proverbial cucumber as he surveyed the scene. "That's the chap who accosted me at the Plunkett house, months ago. Said he was the butler, but I never believed him."

"Eddie 'Asparagus' Murkin, now deceased," I said, poking his lifeless form with the tip of my boot.

"You appear to have killed him," the Professor observed. "Judging by the blood. I take it that's his and not yours?"

"All his. I'm fine, just a little winded. It was a long run."

"Your, ah… medical condition is showing." A mischievous smile danced upon his lips.

I am not used to men looking at me in an appreciative way. I will say, in my defence, that my blood was up. I had just run a long way and killed a man. These things tend to have a certain kind of influence. I stepped over the body of Murkin, put my less-bloodied arm around the Professor's shoulders, and kissed him full on the lips. He didn't put up any resistance at all.

"You kiss like a girl," he commented.

"Well, biologically speaking, I am a girl. I just happen to identify more with the trousers."

"I've always found trousers to be highly influential in my life," he replied. "I like to be clear about these things; I find it causes all sorts of problems, otherwise."

I kissed him again, just to make sure I hadn't missed anything. Apparently this sort of thing gets more interesting with practice.

"This is all rather unexpected," he said, hands wandering a little.

I remembered the business with the corset. "No sudden acts of squeezing, please, that was most unsettling."

He laughed. "I was entirely convinced you had socks in there."

"I'd like to be very clear that this is in no way a romantic approach; it's a heat-of-the-moment thing, and you are not to read anything into it," I said, realising that things were acquiring a rather compromising tone now.

When he nodded, I kissed him again. Or possibly he kissed me; it became rather difficult to tell. I had never kissed anyone before today. It was affecting, and not without charm.

Editor's note: I did consider removing this bit for decency, but then I thought long and hard about sales, and decided to take the more academically-responsible decision to keep all of the relevant material in the collection.

§

The Elemental Solution

Finally, the series of Hermetic and Scientific murders have come to an end. In a most dramatic scene yesterday morning, the perpetrators of these wicked crimes were finally uncovered. The Floating Sage of Covent Garden, more normally associated with wisdom and respectability, it turns out was a criminal genius hiding in plain sight. Eddie Murkin dominated the London underworld for many years, his role in the trade of high-quality illicit vegetables well-known but never actually proven. The mystery of his disappearance three years ago is now a little closer to resolution.

The unlikely hero of the hour was none other than the infamous Professor Elemental. His devices, more often associated with slaughter and carnage, were on this occasion employed to good use. John the Retriever was crushed to death by one of the Professor's machines, while Eddie 'Asparagus' Murkin was later brought down in hand-to-hand combat.

Afterwards, kidnap victim Maude Plunkett was able to tell police and reporters alike how Eddie 'Asparagus' Murkin and John the Retriever, the floating mystic of Covent Garden, had been passing themselves off as her sisters for years, in order to use her home as a base of operations for their wicked plans.

Having survived the ordeal of kidnap and attempted murder, Miss Plunkett was able to exonerate private detective Algernon Spoon, who had been in Highgate, awaiting trial for these very crimes. A dazed Mr Spoon was released from custody today, and stumbled out into the daylight, clearly at a loss for words, into the arms of his waiting sister, Alison. It was a touching scene, and we can all rejoice in knowing that justice has finally been done in that most traditional and British way: through the efforts of an upper-class vigilante with a dubious track record.

§

From the Diary of Algernon Spoon…

I read today's news with no small amount of pleasure. At my request, Professor Elemental has agreed to publically take all acclaim regarding the Plunkett case. It serves me far better to remain obscure and unknown. I return to business as usual with a pleasing cash settlement from Maude Plunkett, and, thanks to Alison's efforts, the office is once again a haven of order and calm. No doubt it will not last, for several new clients have already presented themselves. I am tempted by the Mystery of the Missing Mayor, and the request by an insurance firm to investigate an escape artist who failed to escape, taking several members of his audience to an untimely end for good measure. I doubt there will be anything grand in either business, but both seem complicated enough to keep me occupied for a week or two.

§

Mister Hoghmes,

It has come to our attention that, since his famous success with the Hermetic and Scientific murder investigation, you have been playing shamelessly on Professor Elemental's good name. Your new habit of describing the blindingly obvious as 'elemental' has not passed unnoticed. As your friends, we would like to suggest that you stop doing this, as it does you no good at all. Humour is not one of your strengths, sir, and if the comments are meant to be ironic, they miss the mark by a considerable distance. You need a better catch phrase than this, we think.

Sincerely,
Alison and Algernon Spoon

§

Dear Algernon,

Or should I be calling you something else now? I have no idea if you are Algernon or Alison or someone else entirely. I am, however, fairly confident that some kissing was involved, and that you showed all the regular symptoms of femininity at the time. I'd rather like to know who it was that I kissed, if at all possible. I find it helps to keep track of these things.

I fear the airship was damaged beyond repair. Not so much by all the crashing, I think, as by the enthusiastic urchins of London who wasted no time in taking it apart and running away with all the pieces. Geoffrey was able to recover a couple of knobs, but very little else. The minions are running riot, and that could have been a bit awkward, save for the fact that Lord Troutwallop has declared some kind of city hunting season. He's put in a huge order for both badgermingos and badger minions for the express purposes of unleashing them in the streets to see how many paupers they can kill before someone shoots them. I'm not sure about this. It is a lot of money, but a harsh fate for my lovely creations. Apparently it's going to be all the rage for people with money and guns and whatnot. Probably not for the paupers, but that's never stopped anyone before. As you know, I've never been one to court popularity and draw undue attention to myself with silly gimmicks, so it will be rather novel to be the centre of attention in this way. I'm sure it won't last. The badgermingos will undoubtedly pick up the use of firearms or something equally embarrassing, and then it'll be nothing but visits from the police and difficult questions. Such is the life of science, I'm afraid.

I still rather fancy a sideline in criminal investigation. I provide the scientific genius and fabulous devices, you do all the detecting. What do you say? I think we make a rather good team. It would be a terrible shame not to see you again, for work purposes. There's still a hole in the crotch of my love trousers, due to mice, but that may not be an insurmountable sort of problem.

Horatio has gone home. The place seems very quiet, just myself and Geoffrey, a few giant, sinister rodents and whatever it is that's taken up residence in the cellar. Well, mustn't complain. I have badgers to behead and so forth.

Sincerely,
Professor Elemental

§

My Dear Professor,

It was a pleasure to hear from you. I do feel I owe you some explanation, for your own peace of mind at least. However, none of this is widely known, and your discretion would be much appreciated. While it's not the case that a chap has to whip out his willy in order to enter professional life, that might as well be true. Algernon Spoon needs to exist as a man, or life will become unbearable for me. I hope that you can understand this.

Let me tell you a story. Once upon a time there was a woman who gave birth to two daughters. Twins. She was quite alone in the world – already widowed and with no one to help her. Furthermore, she was of a delicate constitution and feared she would not live long enough to see her girls safely to adulthood. She could foresee a terrible future for her children, unprotected and likely to fall prey to unmentionable things and people. And so she dressed one little girl in breeches and had her christened with a boy's name, raised to act the part of a boy. Thus one twin could defend the other, and the two might survive. Such a person as this has never learned how to be a girl, or a woman, and will never be a wife, and had not considered being anything else either, and was rather surprised about the whole kissing thing.

Algernon Spoon is now returned to his normal self, all medical conditions carefully tucked out of sight, and trousers very much at the ready. I am almost sorry that you did not turn out to be my evil nemesis; we are well matched and could have spent many happy years sparring. I have no doubt, though, that our paths will cross again. If my work calls for your unique skills and insights, rest assured that I will be in touch.

Sincerely yours,

Algernon Spoon

P.S., have not kissed anyone else, before or since. Am not quite sure what this means, but find myself thinking about it rather a lot.

§

Dear, Darling Professor,

Loving my lovely, lovely water-slide. Found a badger on it the other day. Splendid. Must take you to lunch with the Hermetic chaps. Trying to decide if that business with the giant robot and the sage ought to give you an elevated score this month. If it does, I shall have an embarrassment of winnings. I want you to make me a thing. Something so splendid that I shall have to change my trousers every time I think about it. What do you say?

Kisses to Geoffrey, and big, manly hugs to your most excellent self. Also, am trying the mushroom diet this month. Never felt better!

Horatio Plunkett

§

Dear Algernon,

You would be surprised by just how unsurprised I am by

Spoon and Elemental
BRINGING MILD ANXIETY TO THE CRIMINAL UNDERCLASSES

your letter and quite how often this sort of thing happens to me. It does reassure me to think that I wasn't entirely confused on this occasion, though. I entirely understand about the wanting to be a man. Getting to wear trousers, not having to sit awkwardly on horses, being able to relieve oneself almost anywhere, so long as it isn't in the middle of a garden party, when everyone wasn't conveniently looking the other way after all... makes perfect sense to me. Must be hellishly awkward with that sort of thing, though. I'm pondering a useful, portable item to solve the problems of lightening the bladder in a chappish sort of way when one lacks the necessary equipment. Something with a pump and a spout, and only a minimal steam-powered engine. Maybe get it to fit in a hat. Lots of tubes. Could have it play tunes at the same time, although on reflection that might draw too much attention.

Must dash, there's some kind of riot going on out on the lawn, by the sounds of it. Might be the Mostly Pacifist Anglicans, ah, no. I've just peered out of the window, and I see that the Anglicans and the Satanists have both turned up at the same time. I've been getting rude letters from both of them. They're shouting at each other. I'm amazed that Lady Satanists know that kind of language, to be honest with you. They always seemed so refined to me. Still, they've not brought any goats this time, so that's progress.

Oh dear. It looks like some kind of truce has been reached, and they're now marching on my house as one angry body of people. Half of them are praying to God and the other half to Satan, and I'm going to have to start praying that no one hears what they are praying because if everyone turns up at the same time this is going to look suspiciously like Armageddon.

If you get this letter, it probably turned out fine.

Sincerely etc,
Professor Elemental

§.

Editor's Notes

The true nature and identity of Algernon/Alison Spoon remains a mystery. Aside from this letter, the generally available evidence suggests that Algernon was indeed a chap, and that no romantic entanglement between Spoon and Elemental ever occurred. Whether there was a sister and whether the sister was present at the defeat of Murkin and John the Retriever remains uncertain. But then there was that business last year when eminent Doctor Marcus Veryblokey, father of six, turned out, once deceased and in autopsy, to have been female. The origins of the Veryblokey offspring provided much speculation but no clear answers.

Clearly these are exceptional circumstances, and we should

not assume that many, or indeed any of our professional men are in fact women in disguise. It is widely known that the weaker sex do not have the brains for manly thinking or the bodies for manly labour and are really just here to act as ornaments, hostesses and mothers. I cannot stress enough the importance of not investigating slightly effeminate professionals on the off-chance of discovering any more of these most unnatural freaks. After all, if we actually had to whip our willies out to enter Parliament or a profession, that would be very awkward.

Not that I am in any way implying that I would have any trouble producing an appropriate six-inch demonstration of my superior gender. It would take a highly-convoluted mind to interpret my relentless critique of the fairer sex as anything other than natural misogyny, which of course it is, and not any kind of attempt at all to cover up for anything. Ever.

Wilberforce Wilfred Williams

Author's Notes

Which have not in any way been proofed or vetted by Wilberforce Wilfred Williams, who is disadvantaged in this matter by being a fictional character.

Although in all fairness it should be mentioned that one of the authors – Professor Elemental – is also a fictional character and the creation of Paul Alborough. As far as anyone has been able to ascertain, Nimue Brown is mostly real.

Almost all of the history and science in the book is total fantasy, which should have been painfully obvious. The issue of cross-dressing women, though, has a lot more history behind it, and Algernon owes a great deal to pirate Mary Read, who was raised as a boy and spent most of her life wearing trousers, too. A lot of the gender and class politics have some relevance to the period as well, although plenty of things have been taken to extremes for the shameless purpose of eliciting giggles.